## 'I'm not its da

Carly reached into
baby up into her ar

'He does not!'

'And his eyes are exactly the same blue as yours.'

'And hundreds of thousands of other people's...'

'But he's on *your* veranda.' Carly looked down at the baby. 'Oh, dear. What if whoever left him doesn't come back?'

'I'm not keeping him!'

'But he's——'

'No, he's not!' Piran insisted, as if, by repeating it often enough, he could convince himself that it was true. What in God's name was he going to do with a baby?

**Dear Reader**

It's Christmas-time again, the season of love and sharing—and on that theme we have included in this, our Christmas collection, four new heart-warming seasonal novels, by internationally acclaimed authors, where romance is very much in the air. And whether this collection is a present to yourself or a gift to you from a loved one, then we hope that these romances will bring joy into your heart at this special time of year.

Wishing you a very happy Christmas.

*The Editors*

**Anne McAllister** was born in California. She spent long, lazy summers daydreaming on local beaches and studying surfers, swimmers and volleyball players in an effort to find the perfect hero. She finally did, not on the beach, but in a university library where she was working. She, her husband and their four children have since moved to the midwest. She taught, copy-edited, capped deodorant bottles and ghostwrote sermons before turning to her first love—writing romance fiction.

# A BABY FOR CHRISTMAS

BY
ANNE McALLISTER

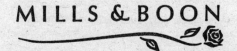

MILLS & BOON

*MILLS & BOON and the Rose Device*
*are trademarks of the publisher.*
*Harlequin Mills & Boon Limited,*
*Eton House, 18-24 Paradise Road, Richmond, Surrey TW9 1SR*
*This edition published by arrangement with*
*Harlequin Enterprises B.V.*

© Barbara Schenck 1995

ISBN 0 263 79281 1

*Set in Times Roman 10 on 11½ pt.*
*94-9511-54110 C1*

*Made and printed in Great Britain*

# CHAPTER ONE

IT DIDN'T even begin to look a lot like Christmas.

In fact as far as Carly could see, when the outboard power boat which served as Conch Cay's only ferry approached the boat dock, Christmas might as well not exist on the tiny palm-studded island with its haphazard rows of pastel-colored houses climbing the hills that made up the one small town on it.

There were no Christmas trees for sale on every corner as there were back in New York City. There was no tinsel garland strung along the eaves of the custom house the way there was in the Korean grocery where Carly stopped every night to buy food for supper. There wasn't even any Salvation Army bell-ringer calling out, 'Mer-r-r-y Christmas,' the way he did every morning right outside the publishing house where she worked so that she felt like Scrooge whenever she passed him. It might as easily have been June.

And thank heavens for that, Carly thought. Actually it was exactly what she'd hoped for, the one—the only— good thing that coming to Conch Cay was going to accomplish in her life: helping her forget Christmas this year.

Most years she started December with fervent hopes for the holiday season. Most years she was a great believer in the seasonal joys espoused by popular songs, even if she'd rarely experienced them in her lifetime.

But this year she didn't want to think about them. Only three months after her mother's death, she didn't want to face Christmas with her stepfather and step-

sisters out in Colorado, even though they'd invited her.
She didn't want visual reminders of how wonderful last
year had been.

Maybe in time she would be able to look back on that
year without the bittersweet knowledge that her mother's
recent marriage to Roland had made her happy again,
but that her happiness had been so shortlived. Maybe
in time she could go see Roland and the girls without
thinking about what might have been.

Not now.

'Come home with me,' John, her sort-of-boyfriend,
had suggested when she'd tried to explain her feelings
to him.

But she hadn't wanted to do that either.

John was far more serious about their relationship
than she was. He wanted marriage.

Carly had nothing against marriage. She wanted it too,
someday. But she wanted love first. She didn't love John
yet. She wasn't sure she ever would. And she certainly
didn't want to increase his expectations about her feelings
for him by letting him take her home to Buffalo for
Christmas.

She didn't want to be in Conch Cay either.

But at the moment it seemed like the least of several
evils. And, if her boss was to be believed, the one that
would at least help her keep food on the table when the
holidays were over.

All she had to do, Diana had said simply, was 'help
Piran St Just finish his book'.

The notion still had the power to stun her.

She hadn't believed it last week when Piran's younger
brother Desmond had showed up in the office. He hadn't
believed it when he'd found out that his ex-stepsister had
turned out to be the assistant editor who'd done the line-
editing on their last book.

But it had taken him barely two minutes to turn the circumstances to his advantage.

'Fate,' Des had proclaimed, looping an arm around her shoulders and giving her a hug. Then he'd turned to Diana, the editorial director. 'Don't you think so? After all, who better than Carly to go to Conch Cay and work with Piran in my place? Our sister——'

'Stepsister,' Carly had corrected him quickly. 'Ex-stepsister,' she'd added.

'Not really,' Des said. 'They didn't get divorced. Dad died.'

'That doesn't make us related,' Carly argued, not wanting Diana to misunderstand her relationship to the St Just brothers.

But Diana hadn't been listening to her. She'd been listening to Desmond. He, after all, was part of Bixby Grissom's bestselling duo; Carly was merely an assistant editor.

'She'll do a lot better job than I would,' Des had said. 'And you know how much you'd like a book set in Fiji next.'

Diana had let herself be convinced.

Carly hadn't. Not at first. She didn't want to go to Conch Cay. She didn't want to presume on her past relationship with the St Just brothers. Though she and Des had been quite happy with their sort-of-sibling relationship while their parents had been married, after his father's death, she hadn't seen Des. And she would happily have gone to her own grave without ever having to face his older brother again!

Once, when she was barely more than a girl and her mother had been married to his father, Carly's starry-eyed fantasies had caused her to believe that Piran St Just was her one true love. The mere mention of his name had sent shivers of anticipation right down her spine.

Now the shivers were of an entirely different kind.

'Come on, Carly, be a sport,' Des had cajoled.

But ultimately it wasn't Des she did it for. It was because she loved her job and wanted to keep it.

'You do like working here, don't you?' Diana had said casually, but there was nothing casual about what she'd meant.

'I'll go,' Carly had said at last.

And here she was. About to come face to face with Piran after nine long years. She wondered what he'd thought when Des had told him. He couldn't be looking forward to it any more than she was.

But they would manage because they were adults now. That thought was the only one that gave her solace. In fact it gave her a small amount of perverse pleasure. She wanted Piran to know that she was no longer the foolish, innocent child she'd been at eighteen.

'You sure he expectin' you?' Sam, the ferryman, asked her now as he cut the engine and the boat snugged neatly against the rubber tires edging the sides of the dock. No one was there waiting, except two men sitting in the shade thwacking dominoes on to a table with considerable vigor.

'Absolutely,' Carly said. Of course he was expecting her. Hadn't Des arranged it? 'I'm sure Mr St Just phoned.'

'Mr St Just don't got a phone,' Sam said.

'Not that Mr St Just,' Carly said. 'Desmond.'

'Ah.' Sam's dark head bobbed and he grinned widely. 'Mr Desmond. What a rascal that man is. Where he be?'

'In Fiji by now, I should think,' Carly said. She shifted her duffel bag from one hand to the other. 'But he said he'd call and tell you. To tell his brother, that is.'

Sam clambered out of the boat, took the duffel from her, then held out a hand and hauled her up on to the dock beside him before turning to the two men. 'You, Ben. Mr Desmond, he call you?'

The man called Ben looked up and shook his head, a sympathetic smile on his face. 'Nope. Didn' phone me. He phone you, Walter?'

The other man shook his head too. 'Nope. Ain't never talked to Mr Desmond. But it don' matter,' he said to Carly. 'You here to see Mr St Just—no problem. We drive you out to the house.'

'Yes, but——'

It wasn't a matter of being driven. It was a matter of arriving unannounced. Carly hadn't expected Piran to pick her up. That bit of courtesy would certainly be beyond him. But she had at least expected him to know she was coming!

If no one else did, chances were he didn't either.

Carly felt an increasing sense of unease. She hadn't been unassailed by second thoughts ever since she'd knuckled under to Desmond's pleas and her boss's not so subtle blackmail.

But now those thoughts were multiplying like bunnies.

She licked her lips. 'No one told you I was coming?'

'No, missy, not a soul. We been 'spectin' Mr Desmond all right. Mr St Just, he been yellin' where he is for a week now.' Ben chuckled and shook his head.

'He be in Fiji,' Sam said. 'Imagine that. Don't that beat all? Ain't Mr St Just gonna be surprised?'

Wasn't he just? Carly thought grimly. Which was exactly what she was afraid of.

But there was nothing else to do—except go home. And even if Des weren't half a world away, and even if her job didn't depend on her bringing back the book, she couldn't go home. She had nowhere to go home to.

She'd told Lenny, her downstairs neighbor, that he could put his divorced sister from Cleveland and her three children up in her apartment over the holidays. And since Lenny's family celebrated both Hanukkah and Christmas she was going to be homeless for quite some time.

Carly shut her eyes and wondered if maybe Christmas in Buffalo or in Colorado might not have been a better alternative after all.

'So, you want to go now?' Ben asked her, getting up and moving slowly toward a psychedelic van with the word 'TAXI' painted on it.

Did she? No, she didn't. Did she have a choice? No, again. Though what Piran was going to say when he saw her was not something she wanted to contemplate.

'Let's go,' she said to Ben with more enthusiasm than she felt.

As little as she had been looking forward to the trip and seeing Piran again, she had been looking forward to seeing Conch Cay. And now, as Ben drove her up the hill through the narrow bumpy streets, she looked around, enchanted, taking it all in. It was every bit as lovely as she remembered it. When Arthur had first brought them here she'd thought it the closest thing to an island Garden of Eden she'd ever seen. Nine years later she had no reason to change her mind.

In a few minutes they left the small town where most of the islanders lived and drove up into the lush tropical vegetation that banked the narrow asphalt road that wound back up the hill toward the windward side. Every so often Carly caught a glimpse of a house through the trees and shrubs. In the distance, as they approached the ocean side of the island, she could hear the sound of the surf crashing against the sand.

She watched with a mixture of eagerness and trepidation for the turn-off on to the gravel that would bring them at last to Blue Moon Cottage, the St Justs' home.

'Mr St Just goin' to be that surprised,' Ben said as he finally turned into the rutted gravel track leading up to the house. 'Course I don' 'spect he'll be too mad. You a sight prettier than Mr Desmond.'

Which might have been a recommendation for another woman, but had never been for her, Carly thought.

She still winced inwardly every time she recalled her last painful encounter with Piran St Just. But now, as she got her first glimpse of the ice-blue house among the trees, she turned her back on that memory and drew herself together, mustering her strength, her determination, her maturity.

Good thing, too, for at the sound of the van the back door to the cottage opened and a man appeared on the broad screened-in veranda.

Carly hadn't seen Piran except on television and in photographs for nine years. It didn't matter; she would have known him anywhere.

He was tall, dark and unshaven. His hair was as black as night and wanted cutting, just as it always had. His jaw was hard and firm, and she saw it tighten when he noticed that the person Ben was bringing wasn't Desmond. His scowl deepened, but he didn't look angry. Yet.

Carly took a deep breath and pasted on what she hoped would pass for a cool, professional smile. Then she stepped out of the van, lifted her gaze to meet his eyes, and was chagrined to realize she was glad she was wearing sunglasses so that he couldn't see how much the mere sight of him still affected her after all these years.

'Piran,' she said, grateful that her voice didn't betray her agitation. 'Long time, no see.'

His eyes widened momentarily, then narrowed. The hard jaw got even harder. '*Carlota*?'

Carlota. No one ever called her Carlota. Not even her mother whose fault it was that she was named that!

Her only consolation was that he sounded as if he'd had the air knocked out of him. He braced a hand against one of the pillars of the veranda and she noticed that his knuckles were white.

'You remember me, I see.'

He snorted. 'What in the hell are you doing here?'

'I gather Des didn't tell you?'

'Des?' He frowned. 'What about Des?'

'He sent me. Got my boss to insist, as a matter of fact.'

'What? What are you talking about? Why the hell would he send you? Where'd he find you?' The questions came fast and furious, but no more furious, obviously, than Piran himself. 'What are you talking about? Where is Des?'

'On his way to Fiji?' She meant it to sound like a statement and was mortified when it came out tentative enough to be a question.

'*What*!' There was no question in that exclamation, just pure disbelief. And even more fury.

Carly would have quailed before it nine years ago. Now she drew herself up to her full five feet six, determined not to let him intimidate her. 'Jim Taylor—you remember, your father's old cap——'

'I know who Jim Taylor is,' Piran snapped.

'Well, he bought a new boat and——'

'I don't give a damn about Jim Taylor's boat. Where's Des?'

'I'm trying to tell you,' Carly snapped back, 'if you'll kindly shut up and let me finish!'

Piran's mouth opened, then snapped shut again. He glowered at her, then finally he shrugged and stuffed his fists into the pockets of his shorts. 'By all means enlighten me, Carlota,' he drawled.

Carly took a careful breath, ran her tongue over parched lips and began again. 'Jim bought a new boat. He's sailing it out of Fiji, and he invited Des to go along and——'

'He *went*?' The drawl was gone. The fury was back.

'He said you'd understand that it was too good an opportunity to miss.'

'The hell I would! We have a commitment! A contract! Does he think the book is going to write itself?' Piran stalked from one side of the veranda to the other.

'No, actually he thinks I'm going to help you write it.'

He spun around and looked at her, poleaxed. 'You? *You* help me write it?'

Carly heard a soft chuckle and was suddenly aware that Ben was still there listening. No doubt the whole island would be hearing about this before nightfall.

'Let's not discuss this out here,' she said in a low tone. 'Let me get my bag and we can discuss it in the house.'

'You're not coming in the house.'

'Piran——'

'You're not! I don't know what kind of stunt Des is pulling, but you're getting in the van and going right back where you came from.'

Carly heard Ben choke on his laughter.

Her cheeks burned. 'Don't be ridiculous,' she said fiercely to Piran. 'I didn't come all this way to have you send me back.' She turned and reached back into the van and grabbed her duffel bag. 'How much do I owe you?' she asked Ben.

'Eight dollar.' He was still grinning all over his face.

Carly ignored the grin. She took a ten out of her wallet and handed it to him. He tucked it in his shirt pocket. 'Thank you, missy.' He slid back into the driver's seat.

'What are you doing?' Piran demanded. 'Stay where you are.'

'Mr St Just gettin' pretty mad,' Ben said as he leaned out the window. 'You sure 'bout this?'

Carly wasn't sure at all, but she didn't see that she had any option. Diana had made herself perfectly clear: when Carly next appeared in the office, she was going to be carrying Piran and Desmond St Just's next best-selling true-life archaeological adventure. Or else.

But she wasn't going to be doing that unless she helped Piran finish it. There was certainly no way she could find Des now and make him take her place.

Besides, she thought irritably, how dared Piran make her seem like some sort of unwanted interloper?

'I'm sure,' she said.

Ben shrugged. 'It be your neck, missy.'

Undoubtedly it would. Carly took a deep breath. 'I'll be fine.'

Ben gave a quick salute and put the van in reverse.

Piran started down the steps. 'Ben! Where the hell are you going? Get back here! Ben! *Ben!*'

But Ben apparently knew that absence was the better part of valor—at the moment at least. The van putted away down the gravel and disappeared around the bend.

It was a full minute before Piran turned from staring after it to fix his gaze on Carly.

'Well, some things never change, do they, Carlota?' he drawled at last, looking her up and down.

Carly met his gaze levelly. 'What does that mean?'

'You're still a conniving little bitch.'

So the battle lines were drawn. It certainly hadn't taken long. If he'd slapped her face with a glove, he could not have challenged her more clearly. Nor could he have found a better means of making Carly dig her heels in.

For a single instant, before he called her that...that— she couldn't even let herself think about what he'd called her!—she'd almost felt sorry for Piran St Just. She'd almost regretted that his brother had deserted him, regretted that he'd have to make do with her help, not Des's.

But when he threw those words at her she thought, Serves him right, damned judgmental jerk.

She supposed she was a bit of a jerk, too, for having thought even for one moment that they could manage this without problems, that he might have changed his opinion of her.

Once—in the very beginning—he'd defended her. It had been the first time they met and she hadn't even known who he was.

It had happened a month after Carly's mother had married Piran's father in Santa Barbara. She'd met Des at the wedding, but she'd never met Arthur's much heralded elder son. Piran hadn't come to the ceremony, Arthur had said, because he went to university in the east.

But he was coming for spring vacation. Carly was going to meet him that very night. In fact, if she didn't hurry, she was going to be late.

She'd waited to leave the beach until the last possible moment, hoping that the small group of inebriated college students standing by the steps up the cliff would disperse. They hadn't. Instead they'd stood watching her approach, whistling and making lewd suggestions that made her cheeks burn.

She'd tried to ignore them, then she'd tried brushing past them and going up the steps quickly. But she'd stumbled and one of them had grabbed her and hauled her hard against him.

'Please,' she babbled. 'Let me go.'

He rubbed against her. 'Let's go together, baby,' he rasped in her ear.

Carly struggled. 'Stop it! Leave me alone!'

He shook his head. 'You want it. You know you do,' he said as she tried to pull away.

A couple of the other men hooted and whistled. 'I like 'em feisty,' one of them called.

'Please!' Carly tried twisting away from him, but he held her fast until all at once, out of nowhere, a savior appeared.

The most handsome young man she'd ever seen jerked the drunken man away from her. 'Can't you hear?' he snarled. 'The lady said she wants to be left alone.'

'Lady? Who says she's a lady?'

Carly's black-haired savior stepped between her and the drunken student. 'I say so,' he said, his voice low and deadly.

The student gave a nervous, half-belligerent laugh. 'An' who are you? The Lone Ranger?' He shoved Piran hard, so hard that he wobbled himself.

The next thing Carly knew the man was flat on his rear in the sand with her savior standing over him, rubbing his right fist.

'It doesn't matter who I am,' he said. 'Apologize to the lady. Now.'

The man's jaw worked. He spat blood on to the sand and glanced around at his friends. They fidgeted and muttered, but they apparently didn't see much point in fighting over Carly. Some of them backed up the steps. A few moved away down the beach. At last it was just Carly and the two of them left.

Finally the student struggled to his feet and glowered at the lean, tanned man still standing there, his fists clenched.

He didn't move an inch. 'Say it.'

The drunken student's gaze flicked briefly to Carly. He scowled. 'Sorry,' he muttered in a surly tone. Then he fled.

Carly stared after him, shaking, still feeling the disgusting feel of his sweaty, sandy body pressed against hers.

'Hey, you OK?' The young man tilted his head to look into her eyes. He gave her a gentle smile. He had the most beautiful blue eyes and the most wonderful smile she'd ever seen.

'F-fine,' she'd mumbled.

'It's over,' he said, and put his arm around her, drawing her close, holding her gently until she'd stopped shaking.

It should have frightened her. He was as much a stranger as the drunken student. But she wasn't frightened. She felt safe. Cared for.

She remembered looking up into his face right at that moment and thinking she'd found the man she wanted to spend the rest of her life with—the man her mother had always told her was out there waiting.

She stammered, 'Th—thanks.'

He smiled at her and ran his knuckles lightly down her cheek. 'My pleasure. Always ready to help out a damsel in distress.' He gave her a wink, then asked if he could see her home.

And that was when he found out whose daughter she was.

'You live where?' he asked her when she pointed out the house on the hillside.

'The pink house. The great big one. Isn't it lovely? We just moved in, my mother and I. She married a professor——'

'Arthur St Just.' His voice was suddenly clipped and short.

'Yes. You know him?'

'I thought I did,' her savior said gruffly. 'He's my father. I'm Piran St Just.'

Her new stepbrother. The one she'd never met. The one, she quickly learned, who hadn't come to the wedding not simply because he went to school in the east but because he objected so strongly to his father's remarriage.

He thought Carly's unsophisticated dancer mother far beneath Arthur St Just's touch and he made no bones about it. In Piran's eyes, she was no more than the gold-digging hussy who had trapped his unsuspecting father into matrimony.

While Des accepted his stepmother with equanimity, at the same time acknowledging that she wasn't quite what one would have expected Arthur St Just to pick for a wife, the same was not true of Piran.

And once he found out that Carly was the gold-digging hussy's daughter his solicitous behavior and gentle concern vanished at once.

Sue, always optimistic, encouraged her daughter to be patient. -

'He doesn't understand,' she said softly to Carly more than once. 'Piran is young, idealistic, and his parents' divorce hurt him. He hasn't known love himself. He doesn't understand how it can happen. Give him time.'

Over the months to come Carly gave him that—and more. Even though, once he knew who she was, he treated her with cool indifference, she couldn't help remembering the first Piran—the gentle, caring Piran who was really there inside.

She told herself that Sue was right. She saw his dislike as a blind spot, one that time and proximity—and her love—would cure.

Until the night of her eighteenth birthday...when she understood finally just how determinedly blind Piran St Just really was...

She lifted her chin now and faced him once more. 'Think what you like, Piran. I'm sure you will anyway. I'm not going to argue with you.'

'Because you haven't got a leg to stand on.'

'Try not to insult me too much,' she suggested mildly, 'or you'll be doing this book on your own.'

'That's another thing. What's all this nonsense about you helping with the book?'

'I'm Sloan Bascombe's assistant editor.'

'The hell you say!' He didn't seem to believe for a minute that she did in fact work for his editor.

They glared at each other for a full minute. Impasse. There were a myriad emotions crossing Piran's face. Acceptance wasn't one of them. Finally Carly nodded once and picked up her duffel.

'Suit yourself,' she said, and turned to head back down the road toward town.

She'd gone perhaps twenty yards when Piran called after her. 'Tell me what Des said.'

She stopped and turned, but she didn't go back.

Piran stood where she'd left him. They stared at each other now down the length of the narrow rutted lane. His hands were still in his pockets, his jaw was thrust out, but there was a hint of concern—of doubt?—in his expression.

'I told you what Des said. Am I supposed to assume you believe me now?'

He shrugged irritably. 'For whatever difference it makes.'

'None to me,' Carly said with all the indifference she could manage. 'Rather a lot to Des, I gather. He was there trying to get an extension so he could go on the trip to Fiji when Diana told him I'd been the one to do the line-editing on your last book.'

'Sloan did it.'

'Sloan signed it. I wrote it. He has forty writers. He can't do everything for everyone. And I know more about archaeology than he does.' She took considerable satisfaction in telling him that and, at first, she thought he was going to object about that too. But finally he gave a negligent lift of his shoulders.

'Go on.'

'You know the rest. As soon as Des found that out, he asked if I'd come and work with you.'

'And you jumped at the chance?'

'Hardly.'

'You're here,' Piran pointed out.

'Not by choice. Diana made it abundantly clear that my job depended on it. Nothing, believe me,' she added after a moment, 'to do with you.'

'Got over your infatuation, did you, Carlota?' His mouth curved, but his smile was hard, not pleasant. 'Or maybe it's like I thought: you weren't ever really infatuated at all, just money-grubbing like your mother.'

It was all Carly could do not to slap him. Abruptly she turned her back and started walking again. She had reached the main road before she heard footsteps coming after her.

'Carlota!'

She walked faster. She knew she could let him insult her. It would be good for her, cleanse her, wash away all her childish hopes and dreams. But she wasn't going to stand there and listen to him insult her mother!

Heaven knew Sue had had her share of faults. But she hadn't been a bad person. She'd been as idealistic as she'd considered Piran to be. She'd just been far more confused. And foolish. And unlucky—until the last.

Carly was willing to admit all those things. What else could you call a woman who had married seven times in search of the perfect love?

But her mother hadn't been evil. She hadn't been conniving.

Never.

But there was no point in telling that to Piran. She had no intention of defending her mother to the likes of Piran St Just! He could go to hell as far as she was concerned. And he could take his book with him.

'Carlota, damn it! Get back here!'

Carly hurried on. The day was hot and sticky for December. And while she hadn't felt the heat much in the van, now her shirt stuck to her back. Rivulets of sweat ran down her spine and between her breasts into the waistband of her chambray trousers. She shifted the duffel from one hand to the the other and continued on.

Heavy footsteps pounded after her. She ignored them.

'Carlota!'

She didn't turn around. She didn't falter.

'Carly, you stubborn witch, stop!'

A hand came out and snagged her arm, hauling her abruptly to a halt. Fingers bit into her skin, holding her fast.

She tried to jerk her arm away, but Piran wouldn't let go. The pull on her arm was so strong he almost dragged her to the ground. She looked at him closely. He seemed winded. His dark hair clung damply to his forehead. His lean cheeks were flushed, but he was white around the mouth, and he was breathing heavily.

'Let me go,' she said again, trying to pry his fingers loose.

His chest heaved. 'Only if you don't start walking again.'

She just looked at him, making no promises.

His fingers tightened. She winced. He looked at his hand still biting into her flesh and frowned, but he didn't let go. 'We need to talk.'

'I'm not talking—or listening—to anyone who insults my mother.'

A muscle ticked in his jaw. She could almost see the thoughts flashing across his brain, angry thoughts, disparaging thoughts. But finally Carly felt his fingers loosen reluctantly. His hand dropped and he shoved it once more into the pocket of his canvas trousers. He shrugged almost negligently. 'Whatever.'

Carly pressed her lips together. She wanted to rub her arm, but she wouldn't give him the satisfaction.

'So talk,' she said frostily.

Piran drew a deep breath, as if trying to decide where to start. Finally he lifted his gaze and met hers.

'Let me get this straight,' he said after a long moment, and she could still hear his disbelief. 'You just happen to work at Bixby Grissom and you just happened to edit our book?'

'More or less. As I said, Sloan has a lot on his plate, and since I know more about archaeology than he does he asked me if I would do your last revision letter for him and the last line-editing.'

'Which he signed.'

'He's your editor. I'm not. And Des came to see him, but he was out with the flu.'

'So Des just jumped at the chance to suggest you come in his place.'

'I'm sure Des was just there to ask for an extension. But when he saw me a light bulb went off in his head. You know Des and his ideas.'

Piran grimaced. 'Yeah, I know Des and his ideas. What I don't know is why you agreed.'

'I told you—because I like my job. And because I wasn't sure how much longer I'd have it if I didn't. It certainly wasn't because I was ecstatic about seeing you.'

Was that a flush making his cheeks darker? 'I'm glad to hear it,' he said gruffly after a moment.

She waited, the sun beating down on her back, but he didn't say anything else. He just shut his eyes. His jaw tightened.

'So,' Carly said finally, 'do I stay or leave?'

He sighed, then opened his eyes. 'Like you I have no choice. What else can I do if we're going to turn the book in on time?'

'Des said you had a draft.'

'Des is ever an optimist.' His tone was dry. 'I have a very rough draft—the operative word being "rough". I was counting on Des to shape it up. He's supposed to be here,' he muttered again.

'Yes, well, he's not. I'm it. Unless you want to plead with Diana for an extension.'

Piran shook his head. 'It's in the schedule. Promo's being done. You know that as well as I do.' All at once he muttered, 'God, it's hot. I need to sit down.'

And he did, right there at the side of the road, pulling his knees up and dropping his head between them.

Carly stared at him, astonished. Then she bent down to look at him more closely. 'Are you all right? Piran?'

He didn't answer. She could only see the shallow rise and fall of his back.

'Piran, for God's sake, what's wrong?'

He lifted his head. His face was white. 'Nothing.'

'Nothing?' she mocked. 'You're just resting?'

'Just resting,' he agreed, his voice hollow. Carly could see sweat beading on his forehead and upper lip.

'You're sick.'

He shook his head. 'I had a diving accident a while ago. No big deal.'

As far as Carly could recall from the days when she'd been a part of the St Just family, there was no such thing as a diving accident that was 'no big deal'.

'What kind of diving accident?' And why hadn't Des told her? Trust Des to stick her with Piran who was ill as well as harsh, fierce and moody.

Piran gave a quick shake of his head and straightened, putting his hands behind him and leaning back, dropping his head back so that now her eyes were drawn to the long column of his throat, the strong jut of his chin and the quick rise and fall of his chest.

'What kind of accident?' Carly repeated.

'Had to come up too fast.' He sighed. 'Damn, I hate this.'

'Then don't run after people,' Carly said, taking refuge in gruffness. She wasn't about to let him think she was concerned.

Piran's mouth quirked. 'I'll try not to.'

'Why'd you do a stupid thing like that? Come up too fast, I mean.'

'Cut myself. Lost a lot of blood.'

'Blood?' Carly looked at him, aghast.

'Gashed my leg on some coral. Not a bad wound, but there're sharks out there sometimes...'

His voice trailed off. He didn't have to finish; Carly knew exactly what could have happened. She felt sick.

'There were two of us,' Piran went on. 'The other guy wasn't cut, but he couldn't stay down either without me. And they only had one decompression unit. He showed more effects, so they put him in.'

'You could have died!' The words were wrung from Carly in spite of herself. She couldn't have stopped them if she'd tried.

He slanted her a glance. 'Wishful thinking, Carlota?'

She glared at him. 'Sometimes you're such an ass, Piran.'

He looked at her quizzically. 'Am I?'

'Yes,' she said tersely. 'Come on.' She held out a hand to him.

He scowled. 'I don't need your help.'

'Fine. Sit there forever. I don't care.' She turned away.

'Carly!'

When she looked back he was glowering at her. He reached out a grudging hand. She hesitated, then grasped it. And there it was—the jolt she always felt when she touched Piran St Just.

She pulled him to his feet and let go at once.

'Thanks,' he muttered.

'Don't mention it.' She turned away again, but she didn't start toward the house until he did. Then she fell into step beside him, watching him worriedly out of the corner of her eye, half expecting him to topple over any moment.

'I'm all right now,' he said as they reached the veranda. 'I'm not going to croak on you.'

'What a relief.' She waited until he'd climbed the short flight of steps, then she picked up her duffel bag and started into the house.

Piran stopped at the door and turned back to face her. 'I'll work with you, but that's it. You're not staying here.'

'I beg your pardon?'

'You can stay in town.'

'Des said——'

'The hell with Des!'

'Well, fine. You want me to stay in town? I'd be delighted. But you're paying for it. Diana certainly isn't going to give me my expenses for something that's above and beyond my duties. And I'm not about to pay for them!' She was so angry that she didn't give a damn if he still thought she was money-grubbing!

Piran dug in his pocket and pulled out his wallet. He peeled off several large-denomination notes and handed them to her.

'You can take the bicycle. There's one along the side of the house. Leave your bag here. When you find something, send Ben back out to get your bag.' He turned away and he probably would have gone right in and shut the door in her face if she hadn't spoken up.

'No. Not now.'

'Wha——?'

'I'm hot, and I've been traveling since dawn. I seem to remember your father once saying that the St Justs were famous for their hospitality. I would like a moment to catch my breath and have a glass of water.'

At the remark about his father Piran turned sharply and shot her a hard glance. Then he grimaced and rubbed his hand against the back of his neck. 'Oh, hell, all right. Come on.'

# CHAPTER TWO

GRACIOUS he was not, but Carly was every bit as tired and hot by that time as she'd said she was, and she was too annoyed to care what Piran's tone of voice conveyed.

She followed him in.

Nothing inside Blue Moon Cottage had changed at all in the intervening years. The walls were still white and cool. The terrazzo floors gleamed. The white wicker sofa and chairs with their bright blue and green patterned cushions still encouraged her to come and sit a while. The mini-blinds were open to let in the air, but slanted to cut down on the afternoon sun, and the outside vegetation filtered away most of the heat. Overhead a five-blade fan circled lazily.

It was the only place where Carly had spent any time while she was growing up that she remembered missing after they'd left.

In spite of having to see Piran again, she'd been looking forward to coming back just to see if the charm remained. It did. Though whether that was a good thing or not she wasn't sure.

'I know where the kitchen is,' she said to him. 'I'll just get a drink. You can go rest.' He still looked pale.

He ignored her. 'I'll rest when you're gone.' He headed for the kitchen. 'I've got iced tea if you'd rather,' he said over his shoulder, and Carly wondered if he only said it because of her comment about the St Just hospitality.

'Thank you. That would be lovely.'

He nodded, went to the refrigerator, poured her a glass, then poured another for himself. Then he nodded toward the deck on the ocean side of the house. 'You can drink it here or we can go out there.'

'My, you are being hospitable,' she mocked.

Piran's jaw tightened, but he didn't rise to the bait and Carly felt faintly guilty for riding him.

She took her glass of tea and went out on to the deck. The view above the trees was of more than a mile of deserted pink sand beach. The first time Carly had seen it, she hadn't believed it was real. She'd thought Arthur St Just must have had the sand specially dyed and trucked in.

Des had laughed, but Arthur had patiently explained to her about the local corals, about how much time it took for the coral to grind down into the fine, powdery sand, how this sand was pink because that was the color of the coral.

Later that day he'd taken them down to the beach and had even built a sand castle with her and Des and her mother. Piran had come by and looked down his nose at them.

Carly remembered that Arthur had invited his elder son to join them, but Piran hadn't bothered to answer. He'd walked right past them and never said a word.

He wasn't saying anything now either. He stood leaning against the railing of the deck, holding his glass of iced tea, not looking at her, staring instead at the expanse of sand and water.

Carly took the opportunity to study him. He'd been twenty-five the last time she'd seen him in person, lean and gloriously handsome, in the prime of young manhood. Full of charm and charisma and promise.

He'd been working on his Ph.D. in archaeology at Harvard during the year, diving with his famous father during the holidays. And when he hadn't been diving he'd been squiring some of the world's loveliest women to trendy nightclubs and fast-lane parties.

As far as Carly could see, he'd fulfilled all those promises. He'd got his Ph.D. He was now, at age thirty-four, an internationally acclaimed expert in the field of underwater exploration and recovery of artifacts. He and Des had written three books to date about the family's escapades.

Or perhaps, Carly amended, Des had written the books. But it was Piran whom one saw on the televised documentaries. And it was Piran who still had all the charm, all the charisma, and all the ladies hanging on his arm.

She knew she wasn't the first woman to succumb to Piran St Just's incredible charm. And she hadn't been the last, either. She'd kept track of the number of beauties who'd been seen with him throughout the years. It hadn't been difficult.

Piran St Just attracted notice wherever he went. And, as she looked at him now, it wasn't hard to tell why.

He might be older now, but his thirty-four years sat well on him. The smooth, tanned skin of youth had weathered beautifully. The paleness of his complexion at the moment was simply a result of his illness, nothing to do with the man himself. There was a network of fine lines around his eyes, but they only called attention to their piercing blue. Just as the strong bones of his cheeks and jaw and the grooves that bracketed his mouth gave his face a sort of cragginess that spoke of battles fought and won.

Pity he didn't have a potbelly or slumping shoulders, Carly thought. He would be easier to ignore if he weren't so obviously gorgeous.

But from what she could tell the belly beneath the thin cotton T-shirt was rock-hard. And if his shoulders were slumped it was only because of the way he leaned with his forearms resting on the railing as he stared out to sea.

Yes, he'd aged well. Damn the man.

She took another sip of her iced tea.

Piran turned his head to glance at her. 'Finished?'

Carly looked at him across her barely touched glass. 'Not quite. Don't feel you have to entertain me, Piran. Go do whatever it is you were doing before I came. I'll drink my tea and I'll go.'

He hesitated, as if he was afraid to leave her alone for fear she might dig in or something. But finally he straightened up. 'Fine,' he said shortly. 'I'll see you to-morrow morning at nine and we can go over what I've got.'

So saying, he drained his glass, carried it back into the house and disappeared into one of the bedrooms. The door shut with a firm click after him.

Carly breathed far more easily when he was gone. She rubbed her fingers along the soft weathered wood of the railing and rued the dreams she'd once had about making Blue Moon her home—about making Piran St Just love her.

It was hard to imagine she'd been such a naïve little fool.

Well, she was a fool no longer. And it was probably just as well she wasn't going to be living here, given that he still seemed to be able to make her respond to him. She certainly didn't want him to know it.

The only thing she regretted was not getting to spend the time at Blue Moon. It was every bit as lovely as it had ever been. It might be easy enough to give up her dreams about Piran, but it would be harder to relinquish the ones about Blue Moon.

She finished her tea and put the glass back in the kitchen. Then she let herself out and found the bicycle, wheeled it back to the road and climbed on, avoiding the ruts as she pedaled slowly toward town.

Piran listened until he was sure she was gone. He lay on his bed, cursing his weakened condition and the twist of fate that had brought Carly O'Reilly into his life once more.

Only when he heard the rattle of the bicycle disappear into the distance did he allow his body to sag into the mattress and breathe deeply.

But still, he couldn't believe it.

God, what could Des have been thinking of?

Well, there was no point in even asking that question.

When had Des ever thought at all? Smart, clever, witty Des somehow never saw what was right under his nose—which was how much Piran hated Carly O'Reilly. And how much he'd once desired her.

It had nothing to do with liking. Never had. Never would. No, that wasn't true.

In the beginning, the first time he'd seen her, he'd liked her on sight. He'd left his father's house after the first of several fights he and Arthur had had. He'd been fuming at the way his father seemed like a besotted teenager around his new wife, a wife that Piran thought was far beneath him. And nothing had taken his mind off it until he'd spied a lovely smiling water nymph with waist-length dark hair and long, coltish legs.

He'd watched her swim, then he'd watched her come back up the beach and stretch out on her towel in the sand. She'd lain on her stomach looking up at the cliff and the bench where he sat. She'd fidgeted, looked up, looked away, looked up again.

Piran had watched her, intrigued, running over various lines, trying to decide on the best one to use for meeting her, when she'd got up and started up the beach toward the steps that would bring her up to where he was.

And that was when she'd met the students at the bottom of the steps. He'd watched her smile at them. He'd heard them speak, but he couldn't hear what they were saying. She'd smiled again. Then, as they'd closed around her, he'd momentarily lost sight of her. He'd got to his feet quickly and started down.

He'd been furious to reach them and discover a shy, innocent girl being preyed upon by hooligans. He hadn't hesitated to step in.

He remembered as if it were yesterday—the drunken shove, the satisfying smack when his fist had connected with the drunk's jaw, the adoring gray eyes that had looked up into his.

His hands, clenching now, remembered too. They could still feel the petal-softness of her skin as he'd held her briefly in his arms. The same softness they'd felt when she'd reached out her hand to help him up less than an hour ago.

In scant moments he'd become her hero. And he'd wanted to be her hero.

Until he'd found out whose daughter she was.

Then he'd felt as if he too had been duped. Her innocence hadn't seemed so innocent any longer. Her shyness had seemed calculated.

It had made him furious then because he'd seen it for what it was.

Pure animal magnetism. Sexual chemistry. Hormones. Exactly the same things that had drawn his poor foolish father to Carly's gorgeous shallow mother.

Piran was damned if he was going to let it happen to him!

And so he'd stayed away as much as he could.

Probably he'd only seen her half a dozen times over the not quite two years of his father's marriage to Sue. But every time he had Carly had changed. She'd grown more desirable than ever.

Her curves developed. Her eyes sparkled with tantalizing laughter and heady promise. Her lips grew full and tempting, just made to be kissed.

But Piran had refused to kiss them. He wasn't weak like his father. He knew there was more to a woman than a pretty face.

Ever since he was a tiny child, he'd idolized Arthur St Just, had grown up wanting to be just like him. He'd even taken his father's side in his parents' divorce.

In his eyes, Arthur St Just could do no wrong—until he'd met and married, in the space of a few short weeks, the blowsy, beautiful dancer Sue O'Reilly Delgado Gower Tremaine.

God, Piran thought, his fist clenching at his side and pounding on the mattress, even now he could remember the litany of her names!

Carly had told them to him once—recited them, actually, her wide gray eyes watching for his reaction. He'd gritted his teeth then. He gritted them now.

He couldn't believe his father had fallen for a tramp like Sue—a dancer, for heaven's sake! A woman with no education, no background, nothing—except a daughter.

Carly.

Carly, whose laughter and smiles and serious silvery eyes had tempted him increasingly each time he'd seen her, until at last, on her eighteenth birthday, he hadn't been able to resist what she was offering.

Or what he thought she'd been offering.

To his everlasting shame he could still remember how ready he'd been for her. God, yes, he'd been ready! More than ready, he recalled with chagrin even now.

In another few moments he would have fallen completely under her spell. But then she'd opened her mouth and he'd found out that she hadn't really been offering at all. She'd been trading—just like her mother.

Sex for marriage.

Piran might be one kind of fool, but he was never going to be the fool that his father had been. Marriage to Carlota O'Reilly had never been on the cards.

'Marry you? You must be kidding!' he'd said, incredulous. And he'd turned away from her stricken look.

He'd never seen her again after that night. Not even at his father's funeral. He'd missed it, made up an excuse, hating her because he felt he had to, because he knew she would be there.

After that he'd put her—and her mother—out of his mind. He hadn't thought of her in years. And yet the moment he'd seen her this afternoon he'd recognized her at once.

And wanted her just as much as ever, God help him.

'What do you mean, there's no room at the inn?' Piran glowered at her from the doorway. The passage of four hours hadn't improved his mood any, that was certain.

'I was speaking metaphorically,' Carly said. She drooped on to one of the wicker chairs on the veranda, feeling as if she'd been dragged backwards through the mangrove swamp. 'There are no rooms available in Conch Cay.'

'Don't be ridiculous. Of course there are.' Piran shoved a hand through sleep-tousled hair.

To say that he'd been unhappy to see her come back would be something of an understatement.

He'd said, '*You!*' in a horrid voice and fumbled to fasten the top button of his trousers.

Carly had watched with undisguised interest. 'Perhaps you were expecting someone else?' she'd suggested, and fluttered her lashes at him, irritated that he would disbelieve her about a thing like this.

'I was taking a nap,' he'd retorted stiffly.

'Oh. Right. Sorry to disturb you.'

'You're not,' he'd said, which was the absolute truth.

He said now, 'What about Maisie Cash's house?'

'The Potters are there from Phoenix for the holidays,' Carly recited from memory.

'It's not the holidays yet.'

'Tell that to the Potters.'

'Well, what about the Kellys?' he said impatiently. 'They take in visitors.'

'Lots of people take in visitors, Piran. Tourism is the prime industry on the island.'

'I know that. So——'

'So Conch Cay has a bumper crop. It might not look like Christmas out here, but everyone is here to celebrate it. I stopped at the grocery. Old Bill gave me a list.'

'And?'

'And they were all full.'

'You can't have looked everywhere!'

Carly unfolded the list and shoved it at him. 'Then you look. I've looked until I'm ready to drop.' She lay back on the floor of the veranda and closed her eyes.

Piran muttered under his breath. He prowled up and down the veranda, then stood glowering down at her.

Carly opened one eye. 'And don't tell me to go over to Eleuthera and take the launch back every day, because I won't.'

He muttered again and paced the length of the veranda once more. 'I suppose that means you expect to stay here?'

'Unless you have a better idea, I don't see any other option.'

'Go home.'

'We've been through that already.'

Piran made a furious sound deep in his throat.

'What's the matter really, Piran? Are you afraid I'll take advantage of your virtue?'

He let out an explosive breath. 'Maybe I'm afraid I'll take advantage of yours?'

'I didn't think you thought I had any virtue.'

His teeth came together with a snap. 'Don't bait me, Carlota. If you want to stay here, don't bait me.'

'I have no intention of baiting you,' Carly said hastily.

'Good. Remember that. This is work. That's all.'

'You're damn right it is,' Carly said, incensed, sitting up and glaring at him. 'And you're a jerk if you think I want it to be any more than that!'

He met her gaze. 'Just so we understand each other.'

'We do.'

The look went on...and on. Finally he nodded curtly. 'Use your old bedroom. But leave me alone. We can start work in the morning.'

She was surprised Piran remembered which bedroom had been hers.

Or maybe he didn't, she thought when she finally got up and made her way toward the small bedroom next to the kitchen. Maybe he just assumed that she would remember and didn't care as long as it wasn't anywhere near his.

It wasn't. It faced away from the ocean, bordering the narrow drive up which she'd come. The room Piran was using had been her mother's and his father's the last time they'd come here. It was on the other side of the house with access to the deck and the stairs to the path leading to the beach.

Bigger and airier than hers, it also had a lovely view across the treetops toward the ocean. But the small back bedroom with the narrow wicker bed and freestanding cupboard in which to hang her clothes suited Carly just fine.

She opened the windows and got a cross-breeze almost at once. But to aid its movement she turned on the overhead fan. Then she put her things away, slipped off her sandals and lay down on the bed.

She only intended to rest her eyes for a moment. Then she would go out and walk on the beach in the waning summer light. She would dig her toes in the sand and wade in the warm Caribbean water. She would savor the moment and appreciate the parts of Conch Cay she had no trouble enjoying. In just a few minutes she would do that...

It was pitch-dark when she woke up.

It took her a moment to remember where she was. Then it came back in a rush.

Des. Diana. The book. Piran. Christmas. The long trip by taxi, plane, taxi, and boat to Conch Cay. Piran's less than enthusiastic welcome. Her fruitless search for a room. Her return to Blue Moon Cottage. Piran's reluctant agreement to her staying with him. Piran. Always Piran.

Carly rolled over and tried to forget him, tried to go back to sleep because it was obviously quite late now. But she wasn't tired enough to go back to sleep, and trying not to think about Piran only insured that she would.

Finally, after she'd tossed and turned for half an hour, she got up and put her sandals on, then padded through the silent house.

The lights were all shut off and the door to Piran's room was closed. She didn't know the time, but figured that it must be sometime after midnight.

Quietly she slid open the door to the veranda and padded out. A swath of silvery moonlight spilled across the ocean, lighting her way as she went down the steps. At the bottom she found the narrow path that led through the trees down the hill to the beach.

Before she was more than twenty yards along the path, she heard a rustling sound in the brush and saw a dark, slithering shape. Swallowing a scream, she stopped dead right where she was.

There were snakes on Conch Cay. She remembered Des showing her the marks they made in the sand which had looked to Carly like the imprints from bicycle tires. But she didn't know what kind they were and she didn't know if any of them were poisonous.

It wouldn't do to get herself bitten by a snake the first night she was here. Piran wouldn't be in the least bit understanding.

The rustling noise stopped and eventually Carly went on. She moved on carefully now, watching her every step, doing her best to make sure she didn't step on anything alive and capable of objecting.

She didn't notice when the path curved and the beach came into view. She didn't see the lean masculine form that slowly rose out of the water and made its way across the narrow sand beach toward the trail.

She didn't see Piran at all until it was too late, until she ran right into his bare wet chest.

'Ooof!'

'Bloody hell!' Hard fingers came out and grabbed her arms.

'P-Piran?'

'Who'd you think it was? The Loch Ness monster?' His fingers were still biting into her flesh as he snarled at her.

Carly looked up into hard eyes, then down at a shadowed but all too evident masculine nakedness, and finally, desperately, away into the jungle brush.

Snakes seemed suddenly far preferable.

'What the hell are you doing out here?' he demanded.

'G-going for a walk.'

'In the middle of the night?'

'I couldn't sleep.' She tried twisting away from him. 'Let me go.' Finally she managed to pry his fingers off her arms. Then she wrapped her arms against her chest, keeping her eyes firmly averted the whole time. 'I certainly wasn't looking for you, if that's what you think!'

Piran made a sound that could have been a snort of disgust or disbelief. 'You shouldn't be out walking now. It's almost two. It's dangerous.'

'You're out,' she said. Of course maybe that was why it was dangerous, she thought a little wildly.

'It's not dangerous for me.'

'How's that for the double standard?' Carly said bitterly.

'I don't make the rules, Carlota. But I can tell you what they are.'

'I'm sure you can,' she said. 'It's not fair,' she complained after a moment.

'Tell me about it,' Piran muttered under his breath. Then he said, 'No one ever promised that life would be fair.'

'Save me the time-worn platitudes.'

He reached for her arm. 'Come on, Carly. Let's go.'

She tried to shake him off. 'I said, I'm going for a walk.'

'No, you're not.'

'Yes, I am.' It was sheer stubbornness on her part and she knew it. But she was determined not to let him have the last word, not to allow him to tell her what to do.

She wrenched away from him and started down the path toward the beach at a run.

She'd got perhaps five steps when he caught her. With one hand he spun her round, then grasped her around the waist with both hands and flung her over his shoulder.

'Piran!' she shrieked as she pitched head-first, then stopped abruptly as her midriff lodged against his shoulder and she hung flailing upside down. 'Piran! Damn you! Put me down!'

But Piran only turned and strode back up the path with Carly slung over his shoulder like some bag of old clothes.

'Piran!'

She twisted and smacked him, her fists coming into contact with hard wet flesh. She opened her eyes and found herself staring down at a pair of lean, hair-roughened thighs and bare, muscular buttocks. She hit them. Hard.

'Damn!' He twisted and tried to catch her hands.

Carly kicked her feet, kneed him in the chest, then slapped him again, hoping the blows stung his wet skin.

'Stop it! Damn it, Carly!' He made it to the veranda, but he stumbled on the steps, and they both went down, a tangle of arms and legs, cool droplets of water and heated flesh. Carly landed face down between the backs of his thighs. It took only an instant's exposure to the hard warmth of his body to have her scrambling to her feet.

'I can't believe you did that!' she railed at him. 'Talk about cavemen!'

He was slower getting up. He winced as he pulled himself up and Carly noticed for the first time the angry scar on his leg. 'Are you all right?' she asked him.

'What do you care?' He snapped a towel off one of the lounges and knotted it around his waist, but not before she'd had a chance to glimpse definite signs of masculine arousal.

She swallowed and averted her eyes. 'I—I don't, actually.'

'I'm not surprised.'

They stared at each other. Piran's gaze was hard and angry, and any arousal that he might feel, Carly knew all too well, was unwanted.

So what else was new? He'd wanted her nine years ago, and he'd hated himself for it.

She glanced back at him and saw a muscle in his jaw tick in the moonlight. She thought he looked very pale. She felt a fleeting stab of guilt, then squelched it immediately. He hadn't had to carry her! He hadn't had to interfere at all.

She said as much.

'Just my chivalric nature, I guess,' he said through his teeth.

Carly remembered when he really had been chiv-
alrous. That memory, sweet as it was, somehow hurt
more than all the other painful memories did.

'Don't bother,' she said shortly.

Their eyes met and clashed once more. Piran ran his
tongue over his lips.

'Fine,' he said harshly after a long moment. 'Go for
a bloody walk if you want. Drown yourself if you want.
I don't care what you do. I don't know why I bothered.'

# CHAPTER THREE

To say that she slept badly was no exaggeration. It was close to dawn before Carly did more than toss and turn fitfully in her bed, her mind still playing with the image of Piran's naked body and the press of his flesh against hers. When at last she did sleep, her dreams were no less alluring and no more restful.

She was reminded all too much of the night of her eighteenth birthday—the last time she'd been held in Piran St Just's arms—the time she'd found out what he really thought of her.

For years she'd turned away from that memory every time it surfaced. She'd blotted it out as soon as she could because it had hurt so much.

But now she forced herself to remember. She had no choice. She needed to remember if only to protect herself from being drawn once more into the fanciful dreams that once upon a time had brought her down.

She'd certainly had her share of dreams about Piran in the days just before her birthday. She'd been living with her mother and Arthur in his home in the hills above Santa Barbara—the low, Spanish-style house she'd pointed out to Piran the day she'd first met him.

It was indeed a lovely house, built to blend in with the surrounding hillside, its gardens half wild. The latter weren't as wonderful as the wild areas surrounding Blue Moon on Conch Cay, but Carly had loved to ramble through them just the same. She'd loved to sit on the bench beside the bougainvillaea and look out over the city lights and the boats in the harbor at night.

Every night she would go there and sit, dreaming of Piran sitting next to her, of Piran touching her, holding her, kissing her.

She'd never really stopped dreaming of him after their first meeting. Perhaps she'd been foolish—no, there was no *perhaps* about it. She had been foolish. But in those days Carly had been as big an optimist, as big a dreamer as her mother.

And Piran, even though he clearly disapproved of his father's marriage, still fascinated her.

She knew there was more to him than his silent, brooding disapproval. She remembered his gentleness. She remembered his touch. And, even though he was silent and stern whenever he was around her afterwards, she wasn't unaware of the way he watched her.

Carly might not have been sophisticated in those days, but even she knew when a man was interested. And Piran's smoldering gaze was a sure sign that he was. Whenever he came home, or whenever he joined them at Blue Moon or in New York, he watched her with an intensity that tantalized her at the same time as it unnerved her.

Carly watched him too, avidly trying to understand him, to attract him. Even at eighteen and hopelessly naïve in the ways of love, she sensed a connection between them. It was tenuous, but it was very real. It had been from the first moment.

At least it was to Carly. She wanted Piran to see that, too.

When Piran came home for Thanksgiving he watched her. At dinner she caught him studying her out of the corner of his eye. On Friday, when Arthur took them to the botanical gardens, Carly noticed Piran keeping an eye on her.

And Sunday morning, before his plane left for Boston, he even went for a walk on the beach with her. He didn't say anything. They just walked. Every now and then Carly ventured a comment, which was met with a monosyllabic response, as if he was as tongue-tied as she was.

He loves me, she thought, and tucked the words away in the depths of her heart to take out and savor again and again.

They tided her over until Christmas, when she and Sue and Arthur and Des flew down to the Bahamas and met Piran at Conch Cay.

She watched Piran closely to see if he was still interested in her. It didn't take long to decide that he was.

There were more discreet glances. More tense, tongue-tied encounters. Another walk on a different beach.

She wanted to know about the cannons on the headland, and Arthur said, 'Piran knows. He'll tell you. Take her down there and explain to her, Piran.'

So Piran did. He didn't say much all the way down the beach. It was a cool, blustery day and he jammed his hands in his pockets and walked steadily, barely glancing her way. But he was as aware of her as she was of him. She knew it because when the sleeve of his jacket brushed her arm he sucked in his breath and flinched away.

As they walked, she picked up shells, asking if he knew what they were. He did, and Carly saved them. She asked him everything she could think of about the cannons, making their excursion last as long as possible. And finally she got him talking about his courses and his field work in archaeology.

She was fascinated, hanging on every word, wishing that someday she might get to go on a dig or underwater expedition with him. She didn't dare say so. Not yet. But she began to dream.

On the way back he stopped and picked up a piece of something shiny and red. She'd never seen anything like it before. He told her it was sea glass, smoothed now by years of being tossed about in the waves.

'Can I hold it?' she asked.

'You can have it if you want.'

Carly wanted. She put it in her pocket with the shells, rubbing it between her thumb and her forefinger all the way home. She knew that whenever she looked at it she would remember this day with Piran.

She must have daydreamed more than a hundred happy scenarios between them after he went back to school. In every one of them Piran came back and saw at last that she had become a woman. He cast aside the cool indifference or faintly disdainful tolerance with which he'd habitually treated her. He started treating her as the woman he loved.

Carly wanted it to happen so badly that she came to believe in it. It would happen, she decided, on her eighteenth birthday.

And when Arthur got a letter from Piran in March saying that, yes, he would be coming for the Easter vacation, she was certain it was true.

He came. She went with Des to meet him at the airport and for a moment she thought his eyes lit with pleasure when he spotted her there. But if they had the fires were banked by the time he was close enough to shake his brother's hand.

He didn't shake hers. He did, however, look at her mouth with a hungry, almost desperate gaze.

He loves me, she thought again. And she hugged the knowledge to herself, happy beyond belief.

From the moment they met at the airport, he didn't take his eyes off her. Everywhere she went, he watched her. Every time she looked up, he was there.

On the night of her birthday she barely ate her dinner, so aware was she of the dark, brooding young man directly sitting across the table from her. Arthur and her mother spoke to her frequently, encouraging her to talk about her plans for the summer, about the classes she would take at university in the fall. But Carly could barely form words.

Des teased her about the boys who were starting to hang around her, about one in particular whose name she couldn't even remember now. And Carly felt her face burn and dismissed all of them quickly, shooting Piran a quick glance and a small, encouraging smile, not wanting him to think she was fickle. He had to know she had eyes and ears only for him!

She didn't know what he thought. Through the entire meal he never said a word. Still, it seemed to Carly that he smoldered just sitting there. Every time she lifted her eyes, she saw him watching her from beneath hooded lids. And every glance was hotter than the last, inflaming the feelings growing between them.

She excused herself early, shortly after she'd opened her gifts, pleading the tiredness that came from an exciting day.

'Rest,' Sue encouraged her.

'Oh, yes,' Carly agreed.

But she didn't sleep. Instead she sat by the sliding door of her bedroom, waiting until she saw Piran leave the house, as she'd known he would, to stroll the grounds.

He paused on the path for a moment. He stood with his back to her, his legs outlined in faded denim, his strong shoulders flexing under the thin cotton of the pale gray polo shirt he wore. He stared out at the winking lights of the city. Then he turned and raked his hands through his hair. Slowly his gaze went from the lights of the city below to the darkened house where Carly stood unseen.

For a long moment he just stared at her room.

Carly stared back, her heart hammering. She knew he couldn't see her, and yet . . .

Come to me! her heart cried.

He took one step in her direction, then his fists clenched at his sides. His jaw tightened and he turned quickly away to hurry down the path.

Carly swallowed her disappointment, but she understood.

He didn't want to come to her at the house. Not at first. Not until he was sure she returned his feelings. As if there could be any doubt!

She waited until he disappeared. Then, hammering heart wedged in her throat, she slipped out the door and followed him.

There was a small bridge over a ravine partway up the hill behind the house. After the winter rains, a small stream ran down it. But this year there hadn't been a lot of rain and by mid-April the stream had dried up.

Still, when Carly came upon it, the first thing she saw was Piran standing on the bridge, arms braced against the railing, staring down into the ravine as if there were something there worth looking at.

She hesitated, then mustered her courage. What, after all, was she afraid of?

She loved him. She knew he loved her. Hadn't she, less than half an hour ago, seen the hunger in his eyes? Hadn't she seen him take that one small step toward her room?

He spun round, his eyes wide. 'Carly?'

She gave him a tremulous smile, wishing he'd hold out his arms to her. In her fantasies, he had. She started toward him.

'What are you doing out here?' he demanded. His voice was ragged. He turned and braced himself against the railing.

'I came after you.' Wasn't it obvious?

'Why?'

'You know why,' she whispered.

She covered the few yards that remained between them until she was looking almost directly into his eyes. He was only three or four inches taller than she was so her eyes were almost on a level with his mouth.

His lips parted. She saw him run his tongue over them before he clamped them shut in a thin line. He shifted against the railing.

'I missed you while you were gone,' she told him softly.

'Did you?' He stuffed his hands into the pockets of his jeans. 'I can't imagine why.'

'Can't you?'

A harsh breath whistled out between his lips. 'Damn it, Carly, what the hell are you trying to do?'

She probably wouldn't have said it if it hadn't been her birthday, if she hadn't dreamed it so many times that she didn't see how it couldn't be true, if she hadn't trusted him to love her with the same fervor with which she loved him.

But she did, and so she said quite sincerely, 'Trying to get you to give me my birthday kiss, of course.' And she looked up into his eyes and parted her lips expectantly.

'For God's sake, Carly!'

She blinked at his explosive reaction. 'Well, your father did,' she said defensively after a moment. 'Even Des did. But not you.'

He muttered something indistinct under his breath. 'You know what you're asking for?' he said harshly.

She nodded slowly, but deliberately. Of course she knew. She'd dreamed of it—of him—for months.

He stared at her for a long moment, then he jerked his hands out of his pockets and reached for her, hauling her hard against him and taking her mouth with his.

It wasn't that Carly was a total innocent. Well, perhaps she was. She'd been kissed before. By Des. By that boy he'd been teasing her about. By another one or two sweaty-palmed, pimply-faced adolescents who'd pecked her lips like roosters pecking corn.

She'd never in her life been kissed like this.

She didn't feel kissed so much as plundered. Piran seemed more angry than desperate as he locked his mouth over hers. His tongue invaded the sweet recesses of her mouth, seeking, delving, tasting.

And Carly, both shocked and aroused by the force of his possession, hesitated a second, then responded in kind, even more desperate than he was, touching her tongue to his, dueling with him, challenging him.

And while their tongues fought and tangled their bodies did the same. One of Piran's legs slipped between hers, and she felt the soft denim of his jeans rub against the bare skin of her thighs below the hem of her shorts.

He drew her closer still and his knee rode higher, pressing against the juncture of her legs, inciting her further, making her moan and writhe against him.

His hands slipped inside the waistband of her shorts, skimming right down to cup her buttocks as he lifted her into his embrace. It was further than any boy had ever gone with her before.

But Piran wasn't just any boy, she reminded herself. In fact he wasn't a boy at all—he was a man. With a man's hunger and a man's needs.

And as his mouth and hands and knee learned her body Carly was finding a woman's needs inside herself that night. She wanted Piran every bit as badly as he seemed to want her. Untutored though she was, somehow, instinctively, she knew what to do.

She knew how to tug his shirt out of his jeans, how to spread her hands against the heated flesh of his back. She knew how to nip and taste his lips in the same way that he nipped and tasted hers. She knew how to slide her hands round and press them against his chest, how to rub tiny circles against the sensitive nipples she found there, how to make him groan and drag his hands out of her shorts long enough to tug her T-shirt over her head.

'God! Carly!'

'Yes,' she murmured. 'Oh, yes.' It felt so good, touching him, feeling the contrast between his hot skin and the cool night air that caressed her flushed body.

It wasn't cool enough to calm her fevered blood. In fact the sudden touch of fresh air only made her ease closer to Piran, pressing her breasts against his chest, snuggling in as tight as she could.

She heard the quick intake of his breath. His hands sought the waistband of her shorts again, opening the fastener, easing down the zipper. Carly swallowed hard at the feel of his rough fingertips against her smooth skin. His touch was so possessive, so intimate.

And then it became more intimate still. One hand slipped between her legs, parted her tender flesh and touched her growing moistness, making her quiver with a need and desperation she'd never felt in all her seventeen years. She whimpered and pressed herself against his questing fingers.

Piran uttered a low sound deep in his throat, and thrust his hips against her, so that Carly could feel the taut bulge beneath his jeans. She'd never felt a man's erection before. She'd taken the requisite sex-education classes, had tittered and snickered with her girlfriends about boys, had tried to imagine the changes that arousal would make in a man. But she'd never experienced the evidence of that arousal, had never felt the urgent press of masculine power until now.

Sometimes she'd wondered how she'd react. With wonder? With fear?

Now she knew. She felt nothing of fear, only a desire to know it—to know Piran—even more fully.

She wanted to touch him as intimately as he was touching her. Her hands went to the buttons of his jeans, fumbled, then succeeded in undoing them.

He tried to pull her hand away but she persisted, needing to touch him, wanting to caress the silken heat of his flesh.

'God, Carly!' he murmured again, his voice ragged as she did so.

'Am I hurting you?'

'No! Yes! You're killing me! God, I need—I can't— I don't want——! Stop!' He pressed against her, shuddering, his face buried against her shoulder, his hips thrusting against her.

'Piran? Are you all right?'

He groaned. 'No.' He took another shuddering breath. His whole body was trembling against hers. 'God! I'm...sorry. I... Oh, hell,' he muttered.

'Oh,' Carly said faintly. 'Oh, dear.' She felt her cheeks burn as she realized what had happened. And yet she felt an overwhelming tenderness for him and the need to let him know that she loved him all the more.

She smiled at him. 'I can wait,' she told him softly.

'You'll have to,' he said raggedly. 'I can't believe this. I've never——'

'It's OK,' Carly assured him resting her head against his chest. 'I don't mind. Truly. I'm really sort of glad.'

He pulled back and stared at her. 'Glad?'

She lifted her face and met his gaze, nodding. 'To wait till we're married.'

Hard hands came up and gripped her shoulders. 'What do you mean, *married*?'

'Isn't that what you meant? Waiting until we get married?' she repeated, looking into his eyes, which suddenly seemed large and even darker than normal.

'*Married*?' He almost choked on the word.

For the first time Carly felt a faint shiver run through her. 'Don't you want...?' she ventured finally. But she didn't even have to finish the sentence because the look on his face answered her question even before she asked it.

But just in case she couldn't tell he spelled it out for her. 'I never said anything about marriage. Did I? *Did I?*'

'No, but——'

'Marry you? You must be kidding!'

Carly stared at him, pulling away, hastily doing up her shorts, still never taking her eyes from his face. It was as if he was turning into a monster right before her eyes. 'But you—I—we——'

'We're hot for each other. That's all.'

'But——'

'I'm no sucker, Carlota,' he said. 'Just because my father was dumb enough to get trapped by a brazen hussy, it doesn't mean I'm fair game too.'

It took Carly a moment to realize what he meant. 'You think I——' She couldn't even say the words. She gaped at him. 'My mother never——!'

'Tell me your mother didn't set out to snare my old man! Go on, tell me. Better yet, prove it!'

Carly opened her mouth, but no words came out. Piran stood looking at her coldly, daring her.

And she couldn't answer him. As much as she would have loved to deny Piran's accusation, she couldn't.

Sue had in fact pursued Arthur. She'd taken one look at the tall, bespectacled archaeology professor and had fallen in love—at least she thought she had. And she'd made no bones about it. Carly knew it. Even Arthur knew it.

Arthur had been equally smitten. They might have seemed the oddest of couples, but their marriage worked. And, regardless of what Piran thought of her motives, Sue had never been after Arthur's money. She'd been after him.

But Piran wouldn't understand that.

Piran, Carly was beginning to realize, didn't know the first thing about love.

She looked at him as though she was seeing him for the first time. She still didn't speak.

'That's what I thought,' Piran said roughly. 'You can't.'

He zipped up his jeans and tucked in his shirt. Then he reached down and snagged Carly's T-shirt from the ground where it had fallen. He flipped it to her. She grabbed it and held it in front of her breasts.

They looked at each other, and Carly saw her dreams crumble right before her eyes.

'You don't understand,' she said sadly at last and then she turned and walked away.

The sun was high in the sky when Carly awoke. She groaned, knowing that the minute she walked into the living room Piran would be complaining that she was late for work. Well, too bad.

She'd lain awake half the night remembering in detail all the pain of her youthful encounter with Piran. She was glad she had, no matter however painful it had been to relive it.

Now she just needed to keep that memory at the forefront of her thoughts for the next month. Then there would be no chance of her finding herself giving in to her attraction to him again.

She hauled herself out of bed, washed, dressed and padded out into the living room. As she'd predicted, Piran was already there, seated at the computer.

'Nice of you to join me,' he said.

'Sorry,' Carly muttered, shoving a hand through her hair. 'Must be jet lag.'

'There was no time change,' he said without looking up from the keyboard.

'Then perhaps being tossed around after midnight doesn't agree with me.'

'I'd have thought you'd be used to it.'

She gasped at the rudeness of the remark, and at the look on her face he appeared momentarily discomfitted.

But it didn't last. He cleared his throat and said abruptly, 'In any case, if you're really here to work, Carlota, get yourself a cup of coffee and let's get at this.'

He turned back to the keyboard and started pecking at it with two fingers.

Irritated, Carly got herself a cup of coffee. She took a banana too, which she nibbled at while she tried to muster a sufficient amount of indifference to work side by side with Piran for the rest of the day.

But once he'd dished out the morning's ration of nastiness he seemed no more interested in rehashing last night's events than she was. He handed her the material he'd finished with, pointed out the parts he'd particularly wanted Des to clean up, said that she could prove her mettle by doing it in his stead, and then went back to work.

Carly went to work as well. She picked up a stack of paper labeled CHAPTER ONE and started to read. It was fascinating. It read like an adventure story—the tale of his father's belief in the elusive caravel, the older man's determination to find it despite the obstacles that nature, big business and several governments had thrown in his way, and his eventual triumph.

Carly found herself cheering Arthur—and his two sons. And then she looked up and found herself contemplating one of them as he sat with his back to her, frowning at the screen and pecking at the keyboard.

It helped, she reminded herself, that he was ignoring her.

She just wished it all helped more.

For, in spite of all her good sense and all the bad memories she'd dredged up during the night, she couldn't deny that Piran St Just was still a very attractive man.

Nor could she deny that, even against her better judgment, she still felt some perverse elemental pull between them.

Damn.

She watched him now, his head bent over the keyboard as he typed. He was wearing glasses, which gave him a scholarly air at odds with his generally roguish demeanor. Carly had never seen him in glasses before. Another man would have looked owlish and nerdy. Piran merely looked like a rogue intellectual. A very masculine attractive rogue intellectual.

Damn again.

'Here. What are you reading? Don't mess with that. I've finished adding some material I wanted to get in. There's lots to work with. Hurry up,' he said now, turning and shooting her an impatient look. 'I doubt

Bixby Grissom is paying you to sleep till noon then dawdle the afternoon away.'

It was a good thing he talked, Carly thought crossly. Otherwise she might accidentally find herself in danger of liking him again. 'Give it to me.'

He did. Carly carried it across the room and settled into the chair across the room. She started to read, stopped, flipped through the small sheaf of papers, then looked over at Piran.

'This? This isn't anything like what I've just read.'

'You were reading the finished stuff. That's the part Des did in August. What you've got to work on is what I've just given you now.'

Carly stared at the typescript in her hands. She tried reading it again. It boggled her mind. 'You expect me to help you put together an entire book from this—this junk in less than a month?'

So it wasn't tactful; she wasn't wearing her editor's hat at the moment, and frankly she was appalled.

'I expected Des to,' he replied stonily, 'if you recall.'

Des would have had to perform a flaming miracle, Carly thought. Granted, it looked as if the facts were there, but nothing much else was.

Obviously the 'you were there' quality she'd enjoyed so much in their earlier books and in the first chapter of this one had been entirely Des's doing.

She wanted to wring Des's neck. 'I can't believe he did this to me,' she muttered.

'Neither can I,' Piran said tightly.

Their gazes met and held, a combination of distrust, dislike and dismay—and a faint, fleeting hint of camaraderie.

Immediately Piran's slid away and he scowled out the window. Carly scowled at him. Eventually he stretched his arms over his head and his shirt pulled up so that

Carly caught a glimpse of several inches of hard, tanned midriff. Less than she'd seen of him last night, to be sure, but—— Quickly she averted her gaze, not wanting even a glimmer of attractive male to distract her dislike of the present situation.

'We can't do it, can we?' he said after a moment. He dropped his hands into his lap and shifted moodily in his chair. 'It's too much.' He turned his gaze on her. 'Go home and tell Diana you can't do it. We'll return the advance and that'll be that.'

Carly considered the possibility seriously. 'I'd love to,' she said finally. 'Unfortunately I can't.'

'Your job? If money's a problem, Carlota——'

'Money is not a problem, Piran,' Carly said flatly. And she took great pleasure in telling him so. Even though she wasn't making anywhere near the money he was, she was surviving and paying the bills. 'I'm speaking professionally. I take pride in my work. I agreed to do this——' she flicked the manuscript a distasteful glance '—and I keep my word.'

Piran frowned and raked a hand through his hair. 'Yeah, but how? Obviously you're not thrilled.'

'No, I'm not thrilled,' Carly confirmed. 'I'm appalled. But I can't do anything else. And I do have Des's first chapter to work with. I can match his style.'

'You can?'

She met his gaze. 'I can.' She dared him to challenge her, but he didn't.

'So what do I do?'

'Just keep spewing out the facts, I guess,' she said grimly. 'And I'll make a book out of them.'

Piran looked doubtful, but he didn't contradict her. Carly felt doubtful, but she didn't see what else she could do.

'Is this the whole thing? Do you have an outline? A workable one, I mean. Not the one you sent to Diana when you sold her the book.'

Piran shuffled through the files on his desk and thrust a handful of dog-eared pages at her. 'This. Des and I put this much together in August when he came by the site. The *last* time he deigned to show his face as a matter of fact.'

Carly took it and slumped into the chair again. 'Get back to work,' she said.

They settled into a routine. Using the outline, Piran's rough draft and Des's first chapter, Carly did get a notion of where the book intended to go. She already knew from what Sloan had told her that once the adventure part was done this book would discuss life aboard a Spanish ship, a caravel, that had capsized in a storm off one of the smaller Bahamian islands over three hundred and fifty years before.

It was the ship that Arthur St Just had discovered shortly before he died.

Most experts in the field had doubted that Arthur would find it, but Carly, with the faith of the young, had believed in him. She'd desperately wanted to be a part of the search, and she'd always regretted that after Arthur's death she hadn't felt welcome. She'd never expected for a moment to be a part of writing the book about it.

Now, as she pored over the outline and Piran's draft, she felt some of that old excitement returning.

Maybe, just maybe, if they worked flat out they could get it done. And she could prove to Piran that she wasn't just a money-hungry parasite in the process. She would so love to make him choke on his words. She worked all afternoon, sorting pages and scribbling notes, making stacks of paper here and there on the living-room floor, muttering to herself as she did so.

'Well?' Piran said finally, breaking into her reverie.

Carly glanced over at him, startled, to find him looking at her. 'I think we can make it work.'

'You do?'

She nodded. 'As long as you're not going to jump down my throat if I change some things.'

A brow lifted. 'Me?'

The innocence of his tone made Carly roll her eyes. 'Don't tell me. You got an award for sweetness and light that I haven't heard about?'

Suddenly Piran grinned. It transformed his whole face, lightening the usual grim cast of his features, brightening the world, making Carly's heart kick over in her chest. Oh, help, she thought. Quickly she bent down to grab one of the stacks of paper.

'What about——?' Piran began, but she cut him off.

'Shut up and get to work. If I'm going to do my part, I don't need interruptions.'

Piran stared at her a moment without speaking. Then he shrugged and turned back to the computer.

Carly forced herself to concentrate on the manuscript for the rest of the afternoon, reading to herself, muttering under her breath, scribbling changes, scratching them out, scribbling in more and then reading it again. Once or twice she heard Piran clear his throat as if he might say something. She glared at him. He went back to typing.

The only time she stopped was when she heard the sound of a car, then a thump on the porch.

She expected a knock to follow, but nothing happened. She glanced over at Piran, but he didn't even look up. In a few moments the car drove away again.

'What was that?'

'The mail. Ben brings it by whenever the boat docks. Saves me the trip into town.' He didn't even seem to want to make a trip to the porch.

To stretch her legs and get a few minutes' respite, Carly went to fetch it. She found a pile in a small wicker basket by the steps. She carried it back inside. There was some material from the Spanish government, background material which Piran pounced on at once, two journals which he set aside for later, last Sunday's *New York Times*, and one pale pink envelope exuding a fairly potent perfume on which Piran's name was written in loopy feminine script.

He tossed it aside.

Carly was curious in spite of herself. Who was hankering after him now? Was he really that cavalier about the letter or was he just being discreet?

And why should she care anyway? Carly asked herself. Piran's girlfriends were no concern of hers. She took her pencil and started slashing at the second chapter again.

'That bad?'

Carly's head jerked up and she glanced at Piran self-consciously, wondering if he had guessed her reaction to the envelope. His face was unreadable.

'You promised you wouldn't complain.'

'I'm not. But——' he grimaced '—you're going at it with a vengeance.'

'Just making a few notes.'

'You can use the computer if you want.'

'I will at the end of the chapter. I'll put them all in, smooth them out, then you can read over my corrections and make your own. All right?'

Piran hesitated, then he nodded and went back to work.

Imagine that, a civil exchange, Carly thought, heartened. Perhaps they would survive after all.

She glanced his way again, but her gaze landed on the pink envelope near Piran's arm. Who——? No, it wasn't any of her business.

But, whether it was or not, the letter tantalized Carly for the rest of the afternoon. Only when they cleared up for the dinner that Ben's wife, Ruth, delivered that evening did Carly notice that the letter was gone.

Piran never mentioned it. In fact he barely spoke to her through the meal, preferring instead the company of an article from one of the journals that had come in the mail.

'You don't mind, do you?' he asked her.

'Not a bit,' Carly assured him. It was better this way, she told herself. She ate her grouper and salad in silence and tried not to even notice the man sitting across the table from her.

'I'll do up the dishes tonight,' she said when she'd finished. 'Then I'm going for a walk.'

'We're never going to get finished if you're always leaving.'

'I've worked all day!' And she'd fully intended to come back and work for the rest of the evening, but not if he thought he was pushing the buttons.

'So've I. I didn't even rest the way the doctor told me to.'

'So rest, then.'

Now that she took a good look at him, she thought he did look rather peaked, slumped in his chair, poking at his salad. He hadn't eaten a lot, either.

'You won't be any good to Bixby Grissom if you collapse,' she told him sharply.

'The only thing you care about is Bixby Grissom?'

'That's why I'm here!'

Piran grunted.

Carly's gaze narrowed. 'What's that supposed to mean?'

'Nothing.' He turned back to his article.

Carly looked at him a long moment, but he ignored her. Finally she stalked over to the sink, flicked on the faucet and scrubbed her dishes furiously, banging them into the drainer. Then she wiped her hands on the sides of her shorts and headed for the door.

'Be back before dark,' he said as she pushed it open.

'I'll be back when I want!'

'As long as it's before dark,' he said mildly.

She whirled around and glared at him. 'What'll you do—come after me and drag me back by the hair if I'm not?'

He smiled. 'Why don't you try it, Carlota, and find out?'

# CHAPTER FOUR

HE SHOULD have rested. He wasn't kidding about the doctor having said he needed to. But Piran hadn't wanted to get up from working in the middle of the day and take a nap.

It was clear enough that Carly thought he'd done a lousy job on the book. He didn't want her to think he was weak as a kitten as well. Even if he was.

All he'd been able to do was ride her about sleeping in, make her look worse than he did. But she'd certainly worked all afternoon.

If he'd even faintly hoped that she was lying about her role in shaping up their last book, he knew now that the hope was in vain. He also knew that Carly O'Reilly was once more going to complicate his life.

He raked a hand through his hair now as he watched until her curvy little rear end had disappeared beyond the bend. Only then did he move away.

And did he go lie down and forget her the way he ought to?

No, damn it, he did not.

He stuffed his feet into a pair of thongs and followed her down to the beach.

Only because she was such a stubborn little witch that she'd probably drown just to spite him, he told himself as he made his way down the narrow path that wound through the trees. There certainly wasn't any other reason.

By the time he reached the spot where the brush ended and the coral sand beach began, Carly was more than a quarter of a mile down the beach, almost to the point that jutted into the sea.

Piran stopped at the edge of the trees, staying in their shadow, keeping out of sight as he kept an eye on her, not wanting her to look back and notice him.

He was damned if he'd let her think she mattered. As long as she stayed in sight, he didn't have to move.

If she rounded the point, he'd have to follow, of course. But when she got there she climbed up on to the exposed coral shelf and followed it out into the water.

There she sat down and wrapped her arms around her knees. Piran leaned against the trunk of a coconut palm and watched her.

Her hair fluttered out behind her in the early evening breeze and he remembered the way it had done just that the day he'd first seen her.

He shut his eyes, trying not to remember the quickening interest he'd felt in her back then. It was as if she'd been put on earth to haunt him, to mock him, to tease him with the simple love and innocence he'd once believed in and which he'd learned when his parents divorced was really a lie.

Don't think about it, he counseled himself.

And he tried not to. But putting out of his mind the Carly he'd first met didn't mean he could forget her altogether. Instead he found himself remembering her the Christmas they'd come to Conch Cay.

He'd tried to avoid her, but it hadn't been easy. Especially when his father had shanghaied him into taking her to see the cannons and giving her a history lecture. There had been no easy way to get out of it, so he'd gone.

Up until that afternoon, he'd managed to stay pretty well away from her, doing his best to ignore her even though his hormones objected mightily. He couldn't ignore her that afternoon, though God knew he'd tried.

She'd asked a ton of questions and most of them had been good, solid, intelligent ones. She was every bit as bright and inquisitive as he'd imagined her being. And he couldn't help it. Under her questions he'd found himself talking about all sorts of things—archaeology, history, shells. At first he'd managed to answer in monosyllables. But it hadn't lasted and pretty soon he couldn't seem to shut up.

Hell, he'd even shown her a piece of sea glass and given it to her to keep!

He could still remember the warmth of her fingers as they'd brushed his, closing around the glass orb. He still remembered her eager smile, her blowing hair. He'd wanted to run his fingers through it. He'd stuffed his hands into his pockets and stridden on, successfully fighting the temptation.

Then.

He hadn't been so lucky the following spring. His hands clenched into fists at his sides, remembering that night, remembering her touch. He'd never in his life lost control so completely. He leaned his head back against the tree trunk and deliberately shut his eyes.

How in hell was he going to get through the entire month living in the same house with Carly O'Reilly?

Unless...

It would be easy enough, he decided, if she wanted what he wanted—a roll between the sheets.

And maybe she did. She was grown-up now. Maybe she'd wised up and realized that holding out for marriage was pointless. Maybe he wouldn't have to keep his hands off her at all.

The notion made him open his eyes again and consider her speculatively. She'd been no more than a child almost ten years ago—albeit a conniving one. But now?

What if he put the moves on her now? What if he suggested that they might do a little more during their month together than simply writing and editing?

And if she agreed, if they actually had sex, maybe this ridiculous fascination would cease and he could walk away at the end of the month with his curiosity about her assuaged.

And if she didn't?

Or if she did and it wasn't?

Piran didn't want to think about that.


Well, he certainly hadn't taken a nap while she was gone. As Carly came up the path, she saw Piran standing on the deck, leaning against the railing with a glass in his hand, looking for all the world like a jungle cat in wait for his prey.

Well, it wasn't going to be her, Carly thought. And it wasn't even close to dark so he could have nothing to say to her about that. She lifted her chin and didn't even speak to him as she mounted the steps.

He let her pass without comment, then followed her into the house. 'Have a nice walk?'

'Yes.'

'Where'd you go?'

She gave him a narrow, speculative look. 'Down the beach. What is this? Practice in conversational English?' She sat down on the sofa and set the manuscript in her lap, wishing she had a more substantial shield.

'Don't be testy, Carlota. I'm merely making conversation.'

'Why?'

'Why not? We have to live together. We ought to get along.'

'I thought you didn't want to get along. I thought you simply wanted to work.'

'Maybe I've changed my mind.'

She looked at him sharply. 'What's that mean?'

'You used to follow me down the beach.'

Carly's face flamed and her fingers tightened on the pages in her lap. 'There's a non sequitur if ever I heard one,' she said irritably.

Piran shrugged, but he was watching her intently. 'But true none the less,' he said.

Carly shrugged. 'I was young and stupid.'

'Young,' Piran allowed. He came over to the sofa and sat down beside her. Carly cursed herself for not having chosen one of the chairs. She edged away, but he laid his arm along the back of the sofa and his fingers nearly touched her shoulder. She moved as far as she could, hoping he wouldn't notice, but the faint smile that crept into his eyes told her that he had. Her teeth came together tightly.

'Go away, Piran,' she said through them.

'In a bit. Tell me, Carly, how come you never married?'

'How do you know I haven't?'

He looked momentarily taken aback. 'I guess I just assumed...' He stopped, frowning at her.

'I haven't,' she said. 'But it's typical of you, making assumptions like that.'

He frowned, then cleared his throat. 'So, why haven't you?' he persisted. 'You were pretty hot on it once, if I recall.'

'Like I said, I was stupid.' Was it just her imagination, or was he really moving closer?

'I suppose your mother wasn't much of an argument for marriage ultimately.'

Carly's jaw tightened and her fingers clenched. She didn't answer him. She wasn't going to justify her mother to Piran. She knew better than to even try.

'How is Sue?' he asked after a moment.

'My mother died in September.'

He opened his mouth to say something, then abruptly closed it again. He looked startled.

Carly brushed a lock of hair away from her face. 'Thank you for not saying you're sorry,' she said tightly.

Piran sighed and rubbed his hand against the back of his neck. One corner of his mouth lifted in a sort of wry grimace and he shrugged rather awkwardly. 'Because I'd be a hypocrite if I did?'

'Yes.'

'Yeah, well, I'm sure your mother was a fine person...' he began awkwardly.

'Oh, don't!' She didn't want to hear that from him. Maybe when her mother had been alive. But not now.

'I can't even talk about them?'

'Not unless you have something new to say. And you don't, do you?' She met his gaze with a challenge in her eyes.

'It doesn't matter now, does it?' Piran said. 'It's finished. He's dead. So's she.'

'But it's still going on now. Between us. You don't like me because of what you think my mother did.'

He shifted uncomfortably. 'I liked you all right,' he muttered after a moment. 'And you know it.'

'For sex,' Carly said flatly, a tiny part of her wanting desperately for him to deny it.

He didn't. 'You were an attractive girl. You're an attractive woman.'

'Thank you,' Carly said sarcastically.

'What's the matter with that?'

'I'd like to be valued for more than my physical attributes.'

'You're bright and intelligent, too,' Piran said.

She gave him a wary look.

'You're probably going to make a success of Des's and my disastrous book,' he went on.

'I'm going to try.'

'Good. I'll appreciate that.' He smiled at her. There was a speculative light in his eyes that Carly didn't understand fully.

'What?' she said, still feeling nervous.

He reached a hand out and brushed a strand of hair off her cheek. She trembled under this lightest of touches and he smiled again. 'I thought so,' he murmured.

'Thought what?'

'That you still want me.'

'I don't——'

'Don't you be the hypocrite, Carly. You know you do. Just the way I still want you.'

Carly's jaw dropped.

A small, humorless smile played on his lips. 'You're surprised? I doubt it somehow.'

'That's not what I'm here for!' she said quickly.

'Maybe not. But we'd be damn fools not to take advantage of what fate and Des have wrought. Don't you agree?'

And, without giving her a chance to agree or not, Piran leaned forward suddenly, closed the small space remaining between them, and touched his mouth to hers.

It had been over nine years since she'd felt Piran's lips, nine years since her mouth had opened beneath his, nine years since his tongue had tasted her, teased her, tantalized her. Nine long years!

But it might as well have been yesterday. She'd never forgotten.

She'd sought in vain to find that same need, those same feelings with other men. With one of her college boyfriends, with an engineer she'd dated last year, most recently with John. She'd never even come close.

She'd told herself it was just the night, the moon, young love that had caused her fervent response.

Yes, maybe she was a hypocrite, because one touch was all it took to tell her that it hadn't been the night or the moon or young love at all.

It had been then what it was now: Piran.

His kiss was firm and sweet and hungry. And it took her so much by surprise that she responded to it—to him. Her mouth melded with his, her tongue tangled with his, her breath mingled with his. And her heart— oh, dear heavens, what he did to her heart!

She wanted to pull away. No, that wasn't true. She didn't *want*—she *needed*—to pull away. But she was caught, like a fish on a line. And if finally Piran hadn't broken the contact she didn't know when she would have.

'Tell me you didn't like that,' he said unsteadily, his lips still only millimeters from her own. 'Tell me, Carly.'

Carly gave herself a shake, pulled back, licked her lips, tried to still her hammering heart. Oh, God, oh, God, she thought.

'You can't, can you?' he said, and his breath touched her heated skin. 'I didn't think so,' he whispered.

And then he was kissing her again, this time more hungrily than the last. If that kiss had been a test of her responsiveness, this proved that he'd got the answer he wanted.

His arms went around her and drew her to him, and Carly's fingers tightened on the sheaf of paper in her hands, crumpling it.

'D-don't!' she tried vainly, desperately.

But he did. The kiss went on, teasing, tempting, persuading. Piran's hands slid up under her shirt; one flicked open the fastener to her bra with practiced ease, the other moved the thin scrap of lace aside and found the aching fullness of her breast. His fingers stroked and teased, stimulating her, maddening her.

She tried to wriggle away, but the wriggling only made his touch inflame her more. She seemed frozen right where she was. She could only manage words. 'Piran, stop.'

'Why? You want it. Tell me you don't want it, Carlota. Tell me and I'll stop.'

Even as he spoke, his other hand moved to cup her other breast, then to stroke it, arousing it as well.

Carly squirmed against the sofa, feeling the heat of desire curl open deep inside her even as she tried to fight it down. A tiny moan escaped her.

Piran made a satisfied sound deep in his throat. 'I thought so.' His voice was ragged and the color was high in his cheeks. He looked very much the way he had nine years ago—the aroused male, hungry for her.

No, not for her, Carly corrected herself. For a woman. Any woman. There was nothing to do with love in his response to her. It was biology.

And so, damn it, was her reaction to him. She didn't love him! Not the way she once had. Her body wanted him. *She* didn't.

And, realizing that, at last she found the strength to shove him away. 'Get off!'

She wriggled desperately until she fell right off the sofa on to the floor. Then she scrambled to her feet and put the width of the room between herself and Piran.

He shoved himself up and stood looking at her, still clearly aroused and a bit dazed. 'For God's sake,

Carlota, you don't have to act like some frightened virgin!'

What if I told you I am one? Carly wondered, and suppressed an almost hysterical laugh.

She reached behind her, under her blouse, fumbling with the clasp of her bra, trying desperately to hook it again. Piran took a step toward her. 'Stay away from me,' she warned him.

'It's a little late for the outrage, sweetheart. You were panting for me.'

Maybe so, but, 'I'm not panting now, and I'm telling you, I don't want you coming anywhere near me,' she asserted.

'That's not what your body was saying.'

'It's what I'm saying, and I mean it, Piran. You touch me again——'

'Kiss you again,' he corrected her mockingly.

'Touch me, kiss me, anything, and I will be gone on the next boat. And I'll tell Diana exactly why I left.'

She saw his jaw tighten and a muscle tick in his cheek. 'You liked it,' he told her flatly.

Carly didn't answer him, just met his gaze levelly, trying to mask the hurt with outrage, determined not to let him destroy her again.

Finally he gave a sound that was close to a snort. 'I suppose you're still holding out for marriage, Carlota?'

Carly lifted her chin and stared him straight in the eye. 'You're damned right I am.'

Marriage.

God, what did it have to recommend it?

Not a damned thing Piran could think of as he wandered along the beach that night after dark.

His own parents' version had certainly been a sham. What a naïve fool he'd been to believe in it all those years. He'd just thought his parents liked going their separate ways.

How was he supposed to know that for years his mother had had a lover? How was he supposed to know that his father had known it, but hadn't challenged it, preferring instead to bury himself in his work?

It was only when Des was eighteen—'old enough to know what life is all about', his mother had said—that she and Arthur had let their sons in on the truth—and his mother had left to marry her long-time lover.

Good riddance, Piran had thought savagely, feeling betrayed to the depths of his soul. He'd turned his back on her too, determined to align himself with his serious, devoted, beloved father.

And then Arthur had let him down as well.

He couldn't believe it when, just six months after the divorce, his father had called to invite him to his wedding.

'You're getting married?' He'd been appalled.

'I am. I'm in love,' Arthur had said. And even over the phone he'd sounded brighter, younger, happier.

'Who is it?' Piran had asked.

'Her name's Sue,' Arthur had told him. 'She's a dancer.'

'A dancer?' Even now Piran could remember the astonishment he'd felt. He couldn't believe his father—Arthur St Just, BA, MA, Ph.D., D. Litt., Oxon, for heaven's sake—was about to take a nightclub dancer for a bride.

'Don't be a snob,' Arthur had told him.

'Don't be a fool,' Piran had snapped back at him.

He had heard his mild-mannered father's sharp intake of breath, but Arthur had only said quietly, 'I'm going to forget you ever said that. And you will keep a civil

tongue in your head whenever you're around your stepmother, or you won't come around her.'

'Fine,' Piran had retorted. And he hadn't gone to the
wedding. But he hadn't been able to stay away. He'd
gone to visit them a few times—just out of morbid fascination, he told himself. He'd wanted to see Sue and
his father together.

Or had he wanted to see Carly?

He raked his hands through his hair. Then he stripped
off his shirt and plunged into the surf. Maybe working
off his frustration would help him figure things out.

Well, they had certainly determined the boundaries of
their relationship, though to Carly it seemed a pretty
drastic way to do it.

She could still taste him on her lips hours later, but,
if that was what it was going to take to get things out
in the open, maybe it was all for the good.

At least afterwards he'd walked out and left her alone
with her answer: marriage was apparently still not on
the cards for Piran St Just.

Did she really mean that she wanted to marry him?

Heaven knew she hadn't come down here with any
desire of the sort.

And now?

Well, she certainly hadn't proved to anyone's satisfaction that she was over him. On the contrary, he could
still make her blood boil and her heart sing.

But marry?

Oh, lord, why did the thought still tempt her? It
shouldn't. And it didn't make any difference that it did,
she told herself sharply. He didn't want to marry her.

The following day they worked steadily, albeit in
silence. The day after that brought with it a thundering

rainstorm and Piran kept the computer turned off, afraid
to risk having the system damaged by lightning.

It didn't keep Carly from working, but it did mean
that every time she slashed through a paragraph or red-
penciled a line he demanded to know what she thought
she was doing.

'My job,' she answered shortly.

'You're tearing it apart as fast as I write it,' he
grumbled.

'Then write better.'

'I'm doing the best I can.' Outside the lightning flashed
and the thunder rumbled. 'I'm no writer.'

'Tell me about it,' Carly muttered under her breath.
'Now go away. I need to concentrate to make sense out
of this.'

Piran looked affronted. 'It already makes sense.'

'To you. And perhaps to the three or four other people
in the world who have your level of expertise,' Carly
allowed. 'But Bixby Grissom is not an academic publisher, Piran. We're aiming this book at the mass market.'

'And that makes them stupid?'

'No,' she said patiently. 'It makes them generalists.
Your other books weren't this difficult to understand.'

'Thank Des.'

At the moment thanking Des was not high on Carly's
list of priorities. The thunder rumbled again as the storm
moved closer, and, closer still, she heard the car and the
thump of the mail in the basket on the veranda.

'I'll get it,' she said, glad of the excuse to escape even
for a moment.

She brought back in several more journals, some
business correspondence and two more lightly scented
pastel envelopes. She flipped them on to the table closest
to Piran. 'She's an eager little soul, isn't she? Maybe
you'll marry her.'

The moment the words were out of her mouth she regretted them. The last thing she wanted was for him to think she was pining for him.

But he seemed not to notice. He grunted, but left the letters where they were.

Carly scowled at him, then at the letters. Then, heaving a sigh, she forced herself to focus once more on the manuscript in her hands.

The sun came out and set the jungle-like growth steaming. Carly opened all the windows and turned on all the fans but still the sweat ran down her neck and between her breasts. It soaked the waistband of her shorts. The heat was bad enough. Piran prowling around the room made things worse.

'The rain's stopped, so you can type,' she told him.

'I'm composing in my head.'

It looked more like prowling to her. She tossed the manuscript down on the sofa and headed for her room.

'Where are you going?'

'To change. I need a swim.'

'Not alone.'

'Well, not with you.' That was more than she could bear. 'And I'm not refraining from swimming the whole time I'm here just because there's no one to come along,' she told him before he could suggest it.

She went into her room and changed into her swimsuit. It was a very respectable royal blue maillot, its only eye-catching attribute the high cut of the leg openings. She wrapped a towel around her waist and went back out and down the steps.

Piran followed her down.

'What the hell do you think you're doing?'

'Coming with you, obviously.'

'I told you I don't want——'

'And I don't give a damn what you want. It's a matter of safety.'

'I don't need you.'

'I thought you wanted to marry me,' Piran said mockingly.

'Go to hell, Piran.'

But he didn't. He went with her.

Carly did her best to ignore him, practically running down the path, then dropping her towel and plunging straight into the crystalline water, swimming out toward the reef. Only when she neared it did she turn and tread water as she squinted back in Piran's direction.

He was standing on the beach, hands on his hips, watching her. She thanked God that he didn't come in after her. Instead, once he was apparently satisfied that she wasn't going to require rescuing from her own folly, he stripped off his shirt and lay down on his towel.

Carly hoped he'd forgotten to bring his sunscreen. Maybe he'd broil like a lobster.

She swam for half an hour, letting him swelter. But finally she got tired and knew she couldn't outlast him. He would stay as long as she did, and she knew it. So she came out, grabbed her towel, and, without a word to him, began to walk back up the beach to the house.

Piran followed.

She felt naked, walking up the path with Piran's eyes on her the whole time. But she didn't stop and wrap her hips in the towel. He'd only laugh at her if she did.

'If you think wriggling your rear at me when you walk up the beach is going to get me to marry you, you've got another think coming,' he said when they got there.

'You didn't have to come along.'

'Whenever you go for a swim, I'm coming with you,' he replied in a tone that brooked no argument.

'Don't strain yourself,' Carly said. 'Maybe you can find some other watchdog to do it for you.'

Over the next few days she even tried to find someone herself. But no one could. Everyone was busy working and preparing for Christmas.

Christmas.

Well, at least that part of her trip was working. Days had gone by and she hadn't even thought about it.

Until Ruth came and, along with dinner, brought a sprig of mistletoe.

'You don' got a tree,' she chastised them. 'I bring you this. Got it at the grocery store. This be better for you young single people anyway,' she added, giggling.

Carly and Piran both looked at the mistletoe as if it were poison ivy.

'You got to hang it here, see?' Ruth said when neither of them made a move to take it from her. She pointed to the opening between the kitchen and the living room. 'Lotsa chances for kissin', see?'

Carly saw. Piran did too. 'We've got work to do, Ruth,' he complained.

'Too much work not good for you,' Ruth said. 'Here. You come hang it now.' And she wouldn't serve dinner until he had.

'Good. Now the kiss.' She stood back and looked at them expectantly.

Carly looked at her toes. She didn't know what Piran was looking at until all of a sudden Ruth squealed.

'Not me, you dumb boy! You s'posed to kiss Miss Carly.'

'She doesn't want to kiss me,' Piran said.

'Course she does. All us women like to kiss handsome men. Don'tcha, honey?' she asked Carly.

Carly, seeing that sinking through the floor wouldn't be an option, shrugged.

'She says yes,' Ruth translated. 'You kiss her now.'
Piran kissed her.

It was supposed to be a duty peck and Carly knew it.
They both knew it. But something happened. Something fierce, something elemental, something between
the two of them that no amount of common sense ever
seemed to be able to control. One second it was a brief
touch of his lips, and the next it was a hungry, desperate
kiss that asked for things that Carly hadn't even dreamed
of.

'Yeah, mon, that's a kiss all right!' Ruth cheered when
at last Piran let her go and Carly stumbled back, shaken.
'Come along now. I done fixed a box fish for dinner.'

They barely spoke after that. There seemed nothing to
say that wouldn't make things worse.

Then on Friday, while Carly was still working over
the morning's writing, she heard a car and the thump
of the mail on the porch. Glancing at her watch, she
frowned. It wasn't even quite noon.

'Mail's early today,' she said. 'You get it. I'm in the
midst.'

Piran glanced up from the article he was reading,
looked about to protest, then shrugged. He walked out
on to the veranda. Carly muttered the sentences in her
head, trying to hear the way they sounded. She scribbled
some more, then muttered what she'd written.

Piran came back in empty-handed.

'No mail? But I heard the car.'

Piran just looked at her. He was very pale.

'What's wrong?' she asked him.

'It wasn't the mail.'

Carly set down the manuscript and stood up. 'What
was it?'

'A baby.'

# CHAPTER FIVE

'WHAT do you mean, is it mine?' Piran said. No, he didn't actually say it; he shouted it. How dared she ask him something like that?

He paced to the far end of the veranda, then whirled round to glare at Carly. 'I think I'd know if I had a child!'

'Not necessarily,' Carly said so casually that he itched to smack her. 'If you were a woman, yes, of course, you'd know. But——'

'You think I just go around getting women pregnant?'

She didn't answer at once, which made it all too clear exactly what she thought. He scowled at her, then at the baby.

Cripes, a *baby*! He still couldn't believe it.

'Stop pacing, for heaven's sake,' Carly snapped at him. 'You're scaring it.'

Not half as much as it scared him, he thought grimly. But he stopped pacing and watched as Carly crouched next to the wicker basket and peered in at it.

The baby looked back with something akin to worried curiosity.

Piran came to loom over her shoulder and stare down at the infant, too. 'Where do you suppose it came from?'

Carly looked over her shoulder at him. 'Is this a request for a discussion on the birds and the bees?'

Damned if he didn't feel his face begin to burn. 'You know damned well what I mean.'

'Yes, and you know where it came from. The car that drove up.'

'Yes, but who——?' He stopped and shook his head, still dazed. He felt light-headed and this time it had nothing to do with his rapid decompression.

'I should think you'd know that better than I would,' Carly said. 'If you're the father——'

'I am bloody well *not* the father!'

'Then why would someone leave it here?' she asked with maddening logic.

'How should I know? And stop looking at me that way!'

Carly didn't say anything, but she didn't stop looking at him. Piran glared back at her. He could still feel the heat creeping up his neck and he hoped to God she didn't see it. She'd probably take it as a physical manifestation of paternity.

'Just because, once upon a time, you and I got carried away...' he muttered, raking his fingers through his hair.

'Once upon a time? What about when you wanted to go to bed with me just the other day?'

'Yes, well, we didn't, did we?'

'No thanks to you. And don't tell me you've been celibate for the entire past nine years. What about the pastel-envelope lady?'

Piran scowled. 'What about her?'

'Well, she's certainly been trying to communicate with you about something.'

Piran said something very rude under his breath. He didn't want to talk about the girl Carly called 'the pastel-envelope lady'. She was from a time he just wanted to forget. He hunched his shoulders.

'What about her?' Carly persisted.

Piran gritted his teeth. She—Wendy Jeffries was her name—had been pursuing him with single-minded determination ever since he'd met her at a party in Washington a little over a year ago.

He should have known better than to get involved with her, but it had been a hard time for him. His best friend and diving partner, Gordon Andrews, had just died in a car accident. Piran had been driving.

'It wasn't your fault,' Des had told him over and over. Everyone said the same thing. Even Gord's wife—his *pregnant* wife—had said so when Piran had gone to her to break the news.

But being told that he was blameless hadn't helped. Even though the other vehicle had run the red light, he kept questioning himself. What if...? If only... But what had happened had happened. And all the what ifs and if onlys in the world wouldn't bring Gord back.

Piran knew it, but it was hard to accept. He'd done some mind-bending drinking right after it happened.

And he'd met Wendy Jeffries.

He should never have gone to that damned party Des had insisted on dragging him to. And he certainly should never have drunk as much as he did there—or left with Wendy halfway through. He couldn't even remember what had happened after he'd left with her. The next thing he'd known was waking up in her bed the next morning.

His eyes widened and he looked at the baby more closely. Had *that* happened? Was this child Wendy's? Was that what she'd been writing about in all those letters he'd been pitching unopened into the trash?

Had he...? Was he...? God, no, he couldn't have slept with her, could he?

He couldn't remember having slept with her. But then, he couldn't remember *not* having slept with her either.

He felt sick.

He shook his head and frowned down fiercely at the child. *His* child?

The baby's face screwed up and it started to cry.

'Now look what you've done,' Carly admonished him.

'Me? What *I've* done?'

'Oh, poor thing,' Carly crooned, bending closer.

'It's not poor——'

'Damn it, Piran, shut up. Shh, now, baby, Daddy didn't mean to frighten you.'

'I'm not its daddy!' He hoped.

'Piran!' Carly shot him a furious glance. She patted the baby ineffectually. It screeched on.

Piran dragged both his hands through his hair. 'For God's sake, Carly, make it stop.'

'You made it cry.'

'So you can hardly expect I'd be able to make it stop,' he said as reasonably as he could. 'Do something.'

She looked at him helplessly. 'What?'

'You don't know?'

'Why should I? I don't have kids. And I never had any baby brothers or sisters . . . as you might recall.'

'You might've . . . after . . .' But he didn't want to get into anything about her mother. Not now.

'I didn't,' she said flatly.

'OK, you didn't,' he said desperately. 'But hell, you're a woman——'

'Hardly a qualification.'

'Better than I've got. Just shut it up,' he pleaded.

And he breathed a sigh of relief when finally Carly reached into the basket, scooped the baby up into her arms and cradled it awkwardly against her. It wailed, then hiccuped, then sniffled and stopped crying, looking at her with wide, curious blue eyes.

'Thank God,' Piran muttered.

'Try thanking me,' Carly said drily.

'Thank you.' He would have kissed her feet right then—anything just so she made it stop. Why was the crying affecting him so much?

Maybe, he thought, because he wanted to cry himself!
He couldn't be a father! Could he?

Carly pointed to the cardboard box of baby clothes,
bottles and canned formula sitting next to the basket.
'There's a note in there.'

Piran snatched it up. His lips drew into a thin line.

'What's it say?' Carly asked.

'Not much.'

'What?'

'His name.' His fingers crumpled the note.

'Which is...?' Carly prompted.

Piran let out a harsh breath. 'Arthur.'

'Arthur,' Carly said brightly. 'Imagine that.'

Piran gritted her teeth, knowing full well what she was
thinking.

'Hello there, Arthur,' Carly crooned. At that the child
blinked and looked at Carly with more interest.

'He knows his name,' she told Piran happily.

He jammed his hands into the pockets of his shorts.
'Swell.'

'And he has your nose.'

'He does not! My nose isn't beaky.'

'Neither's Arthur's. It's just—um—strong and
determined.'

'Well, it doesn't look like mine. And *he's* not mine.
No matter what that note implies.'

'Don't you think you're perhaps protesting a bit much,
Piran? He's called Arthur, after all. Your father's name.
And——'

'I know it's my father's name!'

'And he's got your nose, regardless of what you think.'
She said this quickly, before he could object. 'And his
eyes are exactly the color of yours.'

'His eyes are blue.'

'The same blue as yours.'

'And hundreds of thousands of other people's...'

'But he's on *your* veranda.'

'Well, he can leave any time.'

Carly stared at him, then looked down at the baby. She made a tiny sound of dismay. 'He can't, can he?' she said after a moment as if the realization had just dawned. 'Oh, dear. What if whoever left him doesn't come back?'

'They'd damned well better. I'm not keeping him!'

'But he's——'

'No, he's not!' Piran insisted, as if, by repeating it often enough, he could convince himself beyond a doubt that it was true. 'I don't care if the note said his name was Piran St Just the second—he's not staying here!'

'How's he going to leave?'

'Whoever left him can come and get him.' He looked around suspiciously, as if whoever had left this baby might still be hiding in the bushes, thinking this was all a great joke. No such luck.

'I think,' Carly said after a moment, gesturing at the large box full of clothes sitting beside the basket, 'that whoever left him doesn't mean to come back.'

Piran had just been thinking the same thing, but he didn't like saying it. With his bare toe he traced the line between the bleached boards of the veranda.

'Of course they will,' he said with far more optimism than he felt.

If they didn't, he couldn't imagine what was going to happen.

What in God's name was he going to do with a baby?

By nightfall Carly was astonished to discover that she had a surprising, heretofore hidden instinct for mother-hood. She wasn't sure how far it extended, but for the

moment at least Arthur seemed to think she filled the
bill.

But if she had a natural flair for mothering, Piran
seemed to have no instinct for fatherhood whatsoever—
beyond contributing the requisite sperm, at least.

He'd watched her and Arthur with a combination of
irritation and nervousness from clear across the room
while she'd fixed lunch. When she'd put Arthur down,
and he'd cried, and she'd suggested that Piran might like
to hold the baby, he'd looked at her askance.

'Not on your life,' he'd said.

When at last she'd set the meal on the table and settled
down to eat with Arthur in her lap, Piran had picked
up his plate and eaten his sandwich at the computer with
his back to them both.

'He's not contagious, Piran,' Carly said.

'And thank God for that.'

He buried himself in his work for the rest of the day.
At least, he called it work. As far as Carly could see it
was a means of avoiding Arthur.

He didn't seem to get much done, either. Mostly he
muttered and glanced at the baby and Carly over his
shoulder, as if he was hoping they'd vanished in a puff
of smoke. Finally he shut off the computer. 'I'm going
to town. Someone must know who the devil he is.'

But when he returned at suppertime he was moving
much more slowly and he had no clues as to Arthur's
identity. There had been a sightseeing boat that brought
forty or so tourists to the island that morning, according
to Ben, including several family groups. No one had
noticed a woman with a baby.

Piran reported all this tersely as he stood glumly at
the water's edge while Carly bounced in the waves with
a gurgling Arthur in her arms.

'So it was a waste of time,' he finished heavily.

'Now what?'

'I don't know. And you aren't supposed to swim alone, if you recall,' he added irritably.

'I'm not alone, I'm with Arthur. Besides, I'm hardly going to drown in eighteen inches of water.'

Piran muttered something under his breath.

Carly looked at him closely. 'Are you all right?' she asked him. His face was red from the sun and the exertion of walking into town, but beneath his heightened color she thought she detected a pale tightness bracketing his mouth.

'Why wouldn't I be? Getting some kid dumped on my doorstep, walking all the way to town and back in the middle of the afternoon, finding out no one knows anything about who he is!'

Carly forbore reminding him that they knew who Arthur was, they just didn't know who'd left him there.

'I know,' she said quietly. 'And you've done all you can right now. So why don't you go take a rest? It might make you feel better.'

'I'll feel better when he's gone,' Piran snapped. Then he sighed and rubbed his hands down his face. 'Sorry. This has just got me——' He stopped and shook his head.

He looked so miserable that Carly felt almost compelled to go to him and put her arms around him. Only knowing that if she did he'd probably only get angrier kept her where she was.

'It'll work out,' she assured him.

He gave her a bleak look, but he did turn and walk back up the beach. He didn't go clear up to the house, though. He stopped instead where Carly had dropped her towel. He spread it out and sat down on it, then turned to stare at her watchdog-fashion the way he always did.

'He'll come around,' Carly said to Arthur. 'I hope.'

Arthur grinned at her and waved his arms.

They played in the water for only another fifteen minutes because, though she'd put sunscreen on Arthur, it wasn't a very strong variety and she didn't want the sun to burn his baby-soft skin.

She stopped beside Piran on her way back to the house. 'May I have my towel, please?' She hoped he would offer to take the baby from her while she dried off.

He didn't. Though he did get off the towel and hand it to her. 'Would you?' She held Arthur out to him.

He backed away, shaking his head.

'Come on, Piran.'

'I can't.'

Carly rolled her eyes. 'He's only a baby.'

'That's precisely the problem.'

'Pretend he's a football. Here.' She stuffed Arthur into his arms before he could stop her, wedging the baby against his chest. 'There. Like that. Hug him close. See? Couldn't you run fifty yards with him?'

Piran looked at her in dismay, his body almost rigid as he held the baby. 'I'd rather run fifty yards from him.'

Carly grinned. 'You're doing fine.'

'You do better,' he said, an edge of panic in his voice. 'Hurry up and dry off.'

Not willing to push her luck, she did just that, then took Arthur back from him. Piran almost sagged with relief.

'That wasn't so bad, was it?' she asked him.

Piran just looked at her.

She hoped he would volunteer to help with Arthur while she took a shower. He didn't. So she took one with Arthur lying on a towel in the middle of the bathroom floor. She dressed with Arthur lying in the middle of her bed. Then she changed him and carried him out into the living room where Piran sat staring at the computer.

'Do you suppose your father was an ostrich in a former life?' she said to Arthur.

'Don't try laying guilt on me,' Piran said without looking at her.

'I wouldn't dream of it,' Carly said lightly. The look he gave her made her smile.

When Ruth came, bringing dinner, she also brought a rattle that her last child had long outgrown, and some bananas for Piran to mash, and lots of suggestions for dealing with a surprise baby.

'I bet you was that amazed,' she said to Piran, smiling all over her face.

'Oh, yes,' Piran agreed in the only case of understatement Carly had heard from him all day.

'Well, he sure be a handsome boy,' Ruth said, looking at the child in Carly's arms. She winked. 'Just like his daddy.'

'I'm not——' Piran began, but before he could say it Ruth grinned and tickled Arthur's bare belly.

'Sure can see that baby done got the St Just nose!'

'Does she think I *want* to claim paternity?' Piran groused at Carly after Ruth left.

'Maybe she just thinks you ought to.' Carly yawned mightily. 'I wouldn't mind if you'd show a little responsibility, either. I'm tired.'

'So'm I.'

'Unfortunately Arthur's not.' In fact he was staring at her wide-eyed and batting at the bottle she was trying to give him. 'Why don't you take him for a while?'

He shook his head. 'You're doing fine.'

'Thank you for the vote of confidence, but I'm tired of doing fine. Come on, Piran. Just for a few minutes.'

She got to her feet, walked over to him and plunked Arthur down in his lap.

'Carly!'

'Relax, Piran. You're fine. He won't hurt you.'

'But I might hurt him!'

'You won't. If I haven't so far today, you won't. Believe me. Just give him the bottle.' She handed him that too.

Piran fumbled with the bottle, finally succeeding in getting it into Arthur's mouth. Arthur took two sucks, then batted it away. Piran looked up at Carly, dismayed.

'Keep trying.'

'But——' But Piran poked it back in to his mouth. This time Arthur glommed on and began to suck. He snuggled down into Piran's arms and sighed.

Piran stared at him, an expression of amazement on his face. 'I'm feeding a baby.' He sounded thunderstruck.

'Will wonders never cease?' Carly said drily. But he really did look astonished, and she had to ask, 'You really haven't ever held one before? Or fed one?'

Piran shook his head. 'I tried once,' he said after a moment. 'When Des was born. I was six. Once I heard him crying and nobody came to get him, so I did.' He hesitated, then went on. 'I'd just got him out of the crib. He was maybe about as big as Arthur—and probably wigglier. My mother came into the room, saw me and shrieked, "Be careful!" and I dropped him.' Even now she could hear an echo of remembered anguish in his voice.

'Oh, Piran!' Carly's heart went out to the little boy he had been. 'You were only trying to help.'

'Yeah. But I wasn't much, was I?'

'She shouldn't have yelled at you.'

Piran shrugged. 'She was afraid I might hurt him. She was right.'

'Was he hurt?'

Piran thought for a moment, then shook his head. 'I don't think he was. He yelled a lot, though. And so did my mother. She told me never to touch him again.'

'It's amazing the two of you are friends now.'

Piran smiled wryly. 'He's taller than I am now. He can stick up for himself. And I need him. He writes better.'

'But you do the hard work,' Carly said. 'The day-to-day stuff. The painstaking stuff.'

'I do what I like,' Piran said simply. 'We work well together because we like different things.'

As he talked he relaxed into the chair and adjusted Arthur's weight in his arms almost unconsciously. Carly, watching him, smiled.

'What?' Piran asked her when he saw the smile.

'I was just thinking that fatherhood becomes you.'

He stiffened. 'Don't start that again.'

Carly perched on the arm of the sofa. 'You really don't think he's yours?' she asked, not wanting to admit how much she really wanted to believe that.

Piran shifted uncomfortably and ran his tongue over his lower lip. 'I don't know,' he said at last.

'How can you not know? Have there been so many women?'

'No, damn it, there haven't. It's just . . .' He hesitated, leaning his head back against the chair and shutting his eyes for a long moment; then he opened them again and looked at Arthur. 'How old do you figure he is? Like six months maybe?'

'I guess,' Carly said slowly. 'I mean, I'm not really good at babies' ages. I'd guess he was born in the summer—June or July. So if you count back nine months he would've been conceived in autumn sometime. September or October.'

Piran nodded grimly. 'That's what I thought.'

'So, the question appears to be who was the flavor of the month last October?'

'There wasn't any "flavor of the month".'

'Well, then you must have some idea. If there weren't hundreds of them. Just think and I'm sure——'

'I told you, damn it, I can't think! I don't know!'

He almost got up, realized he was holding the baby, and slumped back in the chair, a defeated look on his face. Carly watched him, mystified.

He stared at the fan whirling lazily in the ceiling. He didn't look at her. She saw his Adam's apple work in his throat. 'Remember Gordon Andrews?' he said finally.

'Gordon? You mean the boy you went to university with? Tall and thin? Fair-haired?'

'That's the one.'

'Of course I remember him. I met him in New York with you. He was nice to me. A lot nicer than you were. I liked him.'

'You and everyone else,' Piran said, his voice so soft that Carly could hardly hear him. 'Gordon was the best.'

'Was?'

'He died a year ago last August. In a car accident coming back to the airport. We'd been in Washington consulting with a couple of museum staffers, trying to put together an exhibit, and we were almost at the airport and...and a truck...ran a red light.' He stopped and swallowed. 'Hit us broadside. Behind the driver's seat. I came out with only scratches. Des had a broken arm. Gordon was in the back seat. He was killed.'

'Dear God.' Carly felt her own throat working.

'I was driving,' Piran said after a moment. 'I didn't even see the truck coming. I would have stopped if I'd seen him. I should've seen him!' His anguish made his voice ragged. He blinked rapidly, running his tongue over his lips and swallowing again as he stared up at the ceiling.

Carly didn't say anything. She reached out and took the baby and the bottle from him. Then the hand that wasn't holding the bottle reached for his fingers and clenched them.

She didn't say it wasn't his fault. She was sure he knew that—in his mind if not in his heart—just as sure as she was that he still wasn't reconciled to Gordon's death, that he berated himself constantly for not having been able to prevent it.

Piran raised his head slowly and their gazes met. His blue eyes were bright with unshed tears. Then his gaze dropped and he focused for a moment on their laced fingers, then at the child in her arms. A spasm of pain crossed his face and he shut his eyes once more. He pulled away and pressed his fists against his eyes.

'And that's why you don't remember?' Carly said faintly. 'After . . . after Gordon died . . .'

'I didn't cope real well. I got through telling Gordon's wife. I got through the wake and the funeral. And then I just took off. I didn't work for a month. I couldn't. I drank and I threw up and I drank some more. I asked God why the hell it wasn't me. *I* didn't have a wife. *I* didn't have a two-year-old kid and another on the way!' He sighed. 'Des tried to make me shape up, come out of it. He found some girl to get him through it, I guess. He got real involved with her. It seemed to help so I guess he thought I needed one too. He dragged me to parties, introduced me to a ton of them. One of them was your pastel-envelope lady.' He gave her a twisted smile.

And you slept with her? The words stuck in her throat.

'I got drunk the night I met her, wallowing in self-pity, mumbling in my beer. I guess she felt sorry for me.

She took me home with her...and I...and I woke up the next morning in her bed.'

His eyes met Carly's only for a moment, then slid away.

Outside Carly heard the distant sound of waves against the shore and the croaking of frogs near by.

'So...' she began, but her voice wavered. She cleared her throat and began again, 'So you're saying...she could be Arthur's mother?'

'I don't know! I don't remember making love with her! But God, I don't remember *not* doing it either! I don't remember anything after we got to her apartment.'

'What about...? Were there...were there others besides...besides her?'

He rubbed his palms down his face, then rested his elbows on his knees, knotted his fingers and propped his chin on them, looking at the baby in Carly's arms. 'I'm not sure,' he said at last, the words echoing with a hollow, aching tone.

Carly could hear his pain, could see it, could understand the circumstances that had driven him after Gordon's death. Piran always cared—he'd cared about her when he hadn't even known her. He'd cared about his father, even when he hadn't understood his father's marriage. He cared too much. And too often he acted before he thought things through.

They sat in silence for a good five minutes. Arthur's eyes closed and his lips stopped moving on the nipple. They parted slightly and a faint smile tipped the corners of his mouth.

'Is he my son?' Piran whispered. Then he looked at Carly, his eyes dark and desperate. 'What am I going to do with a son?'

# CHAPTER SIX

THE sound seemed to come from a long way off—miles and years away. A high-pitched wail, rising and falling. Tentative at first, then stronger and more insistent. Finally a fierce, angry demand.

Crying.

A baby crying.

Piran didn't know how long he'd been hearing it. Forever, it seemed. First it was Des, the red-faced infant of his past and of his dreams. And then, as he awakened, he remembered who it really was.

This child called Arthur.

His son?

The very notion sent a shaft a panic right through him. He'd barely slept at all, trying to think, trying desperately to remember. Could he have had sex with Wendy? Was she the only woman he might have done it with? God, this was so unlike him! Indiscriminate sex had never, ever been his style. It was just that Gordon's death had hit him so hard.

A fine excuse that was, he thought grimly. God help him, it was no excuse at all. If Arthur really was his son, of course he'd support him; he'd raise him if he had to. But—Piran rolled on to his back and stared at the ceiling, willing the crying to stop—he just didn't want to have to pick him up and hold him!

He felt so helpless, so inadequate. Even last night when he'd given the baby the bottle he'd felt as if any moment he'd do something wrong.

The crying grew louder. Piran's fists clenched in the sheet. Come on, Carly, he begged silently. You get him.

But Carly didn't come.

Piran dragged the pillow over his head. No good. He pressed his palms against his ears. Didn't work.

Finally he could bear it no longer. He stumbled out of bed and made his way into the small bedroom next to his own. He opened the door and went to lean over the makeshift cot Carly had devised.

'Hey, kid, come on, calm down,' he whispered urgently. 'It's OK.'

But his words had no effect at all. If anything the yelling got louder.

'Shh. Hush now.' Piran bent closer. He rubbed his fingers against the baby's warm back, trying to soothe him the way he'd seen Carly doing earlier.

But apparently he didn't have a mother's—or a father's—touch. In any case, Arthur was too wound up to notice. He yelled on.

Finally, desperate, hoping to God he wouldn't drop this child, Piran scooped the baby awkwardly into his arms.

'Hey! Hey, kid. Quiet. It's all right.' He nestled the baby against his chest, holding him snugly as he bounced lightly on the balls of his feet. 'Shh. Really. C'mon, please. Stuff a sock in it!'

Arthur gummed his bare shoulder, his warm little body pressing against Piran's chest, rocking, and Piran began to walk with him. And that at last did the trick. Arthur gulped, then sobbed, then hiccuped and gulped again.

And at last silence filled the room.

'All right.' Piran breathed the words, a smile lighting his face. 'You hungry? Is that what this is all about? We'll get you something to eat. How 'bout that?'

He started toward the kitchen and ran right into Carly.

She jumped back at once. She was wearing only a thin cotton gown that ended halfway down her thighs. Her wild hair was even wilder in the night. She looked gorgeous and desirable as hell. Piran sucked in air.

Then the writhing bundle in his arms kicked his ribs and howled once more, and he had no time to concentrate on Carly or on the immediate stab of lust that he'd felt at the sight of her.

Desperate, Piran thrust the baby at her. 'Here. Do something for him, for God's sake.'

But Carly kept her hands at her sides and shook her head. 'You're doing fine.'

'I'm not doing fine. I've lucked out for the moment. You want the kid to scream all night?'

'He won't if you feed him. You should probably change him, too. He must be wet.'

'Change him?' Piran goggled at her.

She pointed him toward the bedroom. 'You change him. I'll fix a bottle.'

'How about you change him, I'll fix the bottle?'

But Carly shook her head. 'Just be glad I'm doing anything.'

'You're cruel, you know that?' he grumbled.

'A witch, I know. You've told me,' Carly said. She patted his cheek and vanished into the kitchen, leaving him standing there with Arthur still in his arms.

Piran touched one hand briefly to his cheek where he could still feel Carly's touch. Then he looked at Arthur warily. 'I'm supposed to change you,' he told the baby. 'Are you going to yell?'

The answer was yes.

Piran felt like yelling a bit too before he managed to get Arthur out of his tiny yellow stretchsuit, out of his plastic pants and out of his sopping wet diaper, then into another diaper, into another pair of plastic pants and finally into the tiny yellow stretchsuit once more. He felt as if he'd expended enough energy to have salvaged an entire Spanish caravel by the time he was done and Carly reappeared with the bottle.

'Good job,' she said cheerfully.

Piran grunted. 'He peed on me.'

'Occupational hazard. Here.' She held out the bottle to him.

'Nope. Your turn. I did my bit.'

'But——'

'Come on, Carly. Have mercy on me. I've just gone ten rounds with the little devil. You can't expect me to go another five.'

'You're only going to feed him.'

'And give him more strength to battle us tomorrow.'

Carly laughed. 'That's about it.' But then she shrugged. 'All right,' she said, climbing on to the bed. 'Give him here.'

He handed Arthur over to her and she nestled him easily into the curve of her arm then slipped the nipple into his mouth. Arthur didn't hesitate this time. He glommed on to it eagerly and began to suck. His gaze flickered up to meet Carly's and he seemed to say, About time.

Carly smiled down at him. 'That's what you wanted, isn't it?' she said softly. She snuggled him closer and dropped a light kiss on his forehead. Arthur sucked contentedly. She stroked his hair.

And Piran, watching the two of them, felt an odd tight aching sensation in his throat that he'd never experienced before. He didn't understand it, wasn't sure he wanted to. He backed away.

'I'll leave you to it, then,' he said gruffly.

Carly glanced up. 'All right. See you in the morning. Sleep well.'

Piran went back to bed. He lay there and thought about the solid warmth of Arthur's body snug against his chest. He thought about the way the baby had yelled, but then had stopped yelling. He thought about the way Arthur had looked in Carly's arms.

He thought about Carly. About her beauty and her gentleness. About the way she'd looked all those years ago. About the way she'd looked tonight holding the child.

Every time he thought about her he got confused. If she was what she seemed to be, how could she be her mother's daughter?

And yet...she'd make a good mother, he thought.

He didn't sleep at all.

Carly had been up with Arthur for over two hours when Piran emerged the next morning shortly after nine. He didn't look very cheerful. Nor did he look especially rested. His cheeks were stubbled with a day's growth of dark whiskers, his eyes were bleary and bloodshot, his hair spiky and uncombed.

Carly wasn't sure that that was all bad. In fact, she thought that if it meant he had lain awake considering the implications of fatherhood and resolving to face them it might be all to the good.

She watched him warily, waiting to take her cue from some sign from him.

He gave her a bleak look and then walked right past where she sat with the baby on the sofa, without even a 'good morning' to her or a glance at Arthur, straight to the coffee maker, and added enough water and coffee for a full ten-cup pot.

He stood with his back to her, bracing his hands on the counter and staring down at the pot while he waited for it to heat.

So much for becoming resolved to fatherhood.

Carly regarded him with increasing irritation. She stuck out her tongue at his back, then turned her gaze once more to the chapter she was trying to read with Arthur's help.

She noted but didn't look up when Piran left the coffee maker, walked over to the door and stood brooding, staring out into the jungle-like surroundings. She saw but didn't comment when he rubbed his hands through his already mussed hair then stalked back to the coffee maker to scowl down at it and drum his fingers on the counter. She kept her eyes focused on either the chapter or the baby.

When the coffee was ready at last, Piran poured himself a cup without offering her one.

Surprise, surprise, she thought, and nailed him with a glare, then turned back to the baby before he looked up.

He turned, but didn't move to take a chair. Instead he leaned against the counter, staring morosely into the mug that he held against his chest. He sipped once, sighed, then sipped again.

'I don't know what I'm going to do.'

His words dropped like stones into the silence of the room.

Carly looked up to see a desolate look on his face that made her want to go to him and comfort him, reassure him, tell him that everything would be all right.

She didn't do it. After everything that had passed between them she knew exactly how he'd interpret any move toward him on her part. He wouldn't call it reassurance.

Besides, even if it had been in her best interests to reassure him, she couldn't.

She didn't know if everything would be all right.

Looking at the situation honestly meant admitting that there was very little chance that it would be—at least, not in the near future.

Not for him—and not for Arthur.

And for the missing mother, Miss Pastel Envelopes?

Carly didn't want to think about her. She shook her head and looked down at the chapter she'd been reading. Yesterday morning just getting the book into shape had seemed an all-consuming task. Now it hardly signified.

Arthur reached up with the hand that wasn't clutching the bottle and patted her hand, and even though he was the cause of their present difficulties she couldn't help smiling at him.

'All finished?' she asked. But when she started to take the bottle away from him his face screwed up as if he might cry. Quickly she put the nipple back in his mouth and he began to suck eagerly once more.

'Faker,' she chided him.

Out of the corner of her eye she saw Piran's bare feet come a step closer, then stop. She glanced up. His gaze was still bleak, but he was looking interested in what was happening.

'I think,' she said carefully, 'that if you just take things one day at a time it will sort itself out.'

'Who gave you the ability to forecast the future?'

His sarcasm stung and she looked away sharply, pressing her lips together in a tight line.

'Ah, hell, I'm sorry,' he muttered after a moment. 'It's not your fault. I shouldn't take it out on you.' He looked at her, abashed. Then he shut his eyes and shook his head. 'Maybe you're right. But God . . . a baby!'

'Don't think of him as a baby. Think of him as a person, as Arthur.'

'Stupid name for a kid.'

'What would you have named him?'

Piran shoved his hands into his pockets. 'I've never thought about it. Having kids was never high on my list of priorities,' he said after a moment.

Obviously not, since marriage wasn't high on it either. Still, Carly felt compelled to say, 'Priorities have a way of shifting.'

'Don't they just?' Piran took another swallow of coffee and stared out the window once more.

'I was...wondering,' Carly ventured after a moment, not quite sure how to phrase this without bringing his wrath down on her again.

'About what?' he said when she couldn't figure out how to continue.

'Um, those letters?' He didn't look pleased, so she hurried on. 'I mean, if she's been writing you all the time, surely she must've said something, or hinted at least?'

'I didn't read them.'

Carly goggled at him.

'There was nothing Wendy—that's her name—had to say that I wanted to read.' He rubbed his palms down his face. 'At least, I didn't think there was,' he added ruefully.

Carly considered that, actually finding that his admission made her feel better. She didn't want to think about why. 'Where are they?'

'I threw them out. And don't tell me to go get 'em 'cause Ruth took the trash with her when she went home last night. Believe me, I already looked.'

'But——' But clearly there was no recovering the letters. Carly sighed. 'Well, maybe when you get a letter today...'

'Maybe,' Piran said, a hint of hope in his tone.

But, perversely enough, when the mail arrived there was no pastel-colored envelope. There was no letter from Wendy at all, pastel or otherwise.

Nor was there a letter the day after or the day after that.

Piran practically pounced on the mail each afternoon, but, though he blustered and fumed when it arrived, an entire week went by and he never managed to conjure up a pastel envelope.

Carly supposed it was the result of sheer panic and desperation, but they got a lot of work done, even with Arthur there. Maybe it was because they took advantage of every possible moment, or maybe it was simply that Arthur was an easy enough baby to become a part of the routine quickly; whatever, the book was certainly moving along.

And Carly, who'd had virtually no experience with babies before, seemed truly to have a natural instinct for motherhood. Either that or her job had prepared her.

'I think it's the editing,' she told Piran one afternoon.

He gaped at her. '*Editing* prepared you for motherhood? How?'

'The ability to do seven things at once, I think.' Carly grinned. 'There was always more to do than Sloan could handle, so he'd give me one job and before I got ten minutes into that he'd have another one for me. I learned to juggle. Besides that, I learned to placate fractious, temperamental authors. There's not a lot of difference between some of them and Arthur at his worst.'

She said this while balancing Arthur on one hip and stirring the spaghetti sauce that was left over from last night's supper. On the counter next to the stove was the current bit of Piran's writing that she was polishing up. Periodically she glanced over at it, read a bit, set down the spoon, shifted Arthur, and made notes in the margin.

'I never noticed you going out of your way to placate me,' Piran said gruffly.

'Perhaps not,' Carly allowed. 'But in the circumstances I'm sure you can understand why.'

'Maybe,' he muttered. But his tone wasn't quite as sarcastic as it usually was. In fact he'd been fairly silent on all fronts the last few days.

Carly supposed that finding out he had a son was a bit of a jolt—something he still hadn't completely assimilated. They'd had Arthur almost a week and Piran still wasn't really comfortable with him. He gave the baby a bottle every day because Carly said she needed a break. And he changed him, grumbling as he did so, when Carly claimed to be right in the middle of a very important piece of work.

But he wouldn't let her leave Arthur with him alone.

'I'm not ready for that,' he told her whenever she suggested taking a walk by herself or going into town.

And, sucker that she was, Carly caved in.

She was no expert at child care certainly, but she didn't worry about being perfect at it the way Piran did. She'd always learned by doing anyway, and Arthur was a good teacher. If she didn't fulfill his needs, he let her know. If he was wet, he fussed. If he was hungry, he cried. If he wanted attention, he found ways of getting it.

And in one way he'd made her life easier.

Seeing her with Arthur had apparently put a damper on Piran's sexual appetite. Or if it hadn't it had clearly switched away from her for, now that Arthur had arrived, Piran didn't say another word about getting her into bed.

Holding Arthur, she decided, was as effective as holding a can of Mace.

She held him now and studied the back of Piran's head as he sat at the computer trying to work. He didn't seem to be getting very far, if the amount of muttering and blocking and deleting he was doing was any indication.

She had to give him credit—he'd been working like fury since Arthur had arrived—as much to avoid the baby as to get the book done, she suspected. But he looked like hell. He needed a break—an afternoon off. However, Carly had had no luck at all in getting him to take one.

'You want the book done, don't you?' he snapped whenever she suggested it.

And of course she did. But not at the expense of his health. Besides, the book would be done. Of that she was certain.

'But he needs a break,' she told Arthur in a soft voice so that Piran didn't hear her. 'And you're going to have to see that he takes one.'

Arthur looked at her wide-eyed and waved his arms.

'I'll help you.' She carried him into the kitchen, peered into the fridge, spied the milk bottle with only a cup or so in it, considered her options and poured it down the drain.

Then, shifting the baby to her other hip, she went back into the living room.

'We're out of milk,' she said.

Piran frowned. 'None?'

'Nope. And I don't know if Ruth will be bringing any so I'll go into town and get some.'

'I'll go.'

'No. I will.'

'Fine, if you take Arthur.'

'I'm not taking Arthur.'

'But——'

'Piran, it's almost a hundred degrees in the shade. And the humidity is awful. I'm not going to lug him all the way to town.'

'Then let me go.'

'No. I need a break. You'll be fine, both of you.' And, so saying, she plopped Arthur into his lap.

'Carly! I'm working!'

'He can help you.' She stuffed her feet into her sandals and fled toward the door.

'Wait!'

'See you by suppertime,' she called over her shoulder, and vanished down the trail before he could stop her.

It was beginning to look a lot more like Christmas.

Even on tiny Conch Cay.

Sutters' fruit store had a dusting of artificial snow in the corners of each pane of window glass. Cash's hardware and video store had a small sleigh crafted out of spare auto parts perched precariously on the tin roof. There were half a dozen strings of colored lights winking brightly all along the eaves of the government building even in broad daylight. There was even a wreath made of coconut palm fronds and bougainvillaea flowers hanging on the jail-house door.

In the yard of the church she saw a life-size manger scene, complete with a shepherd, three magi, a couple of cracked plastic sheep which had clearly seen better days and a real-live donkey who lifted his head a moment as Carly stopped outside the gate, then went back to cropping the grass. Several chickens clucked around him, and a mongrel dog slept in the shade cast by Mary and Joseph.

There was no baby. It didn't even look as if one was expected.

Rather like Arthur, she thought.

And then she thought, This will be Arthur's first Christmas. And suddenly she wanted to celebrate the holiday after all.

She knew Arthur wouldn't remember it, so in that sense it wouldn't really matter. But at the same time she was sure it mattered a great deal.

Whether he remembered or not, Carly felt it was important to mark the occasion for him, to welcome him into the world, into the family—even as unexpected as he was, perhaps *because* he was as unexpected as he was.

It wasn't her place to do so, she supposed. But maybe, as an ex-stepsister of his probable father, she could argue that she had the right.

She smiled ruefully when she realized how much she wanted the right. She might only have known Arthur a week or so, but he mattered to her. She was going to have trouble letting him go. The thought of losing him so quickly gave her heart a twist that she wasn't expecting.

It should be no big surprise, she reminded herself. Her entire life had been spent in short-term relationships. This would just be another one.

But maybe a few more bittersweet Christmas memories would help both of them.

Maybe they would help Piran, too.

Piran had never felt so responsible in his life. Nor so inadequate. Not when he couldn't hold his parents' marriage together, not when he couldn't talk his father out of marrying Carly's mother. Not even when Gordon had died.

He knew, intellectually if not emotionally, that he wasn't responsible for his parents' divorce or his father's remarriage or even for Gordon's death.

He was responsible for Arthur. Now and forever. Past, present and future.

He was the reason that Arthur existed at all.

He hadn't wanted to believe it. Heaven knew he hadn't wanted a child—not now and certainly not like this—unplanned and unexpected.

But, oddly enough, now that he had Arthur, he found stirrings inside that he'd never felt before.

They weren't merely signs of academic interest as he'd told himself at first. They were something more. Something basic, elemental. They were so foreign, they scared him. Arthur scared him.

And yet Arthur fascinated him too.

He was so resilient, so cheerful. His whole world had been turned upside down by whoever was his mother—Wendy, Piran guessed. And yet he smiled and cooed and snuggled up to Carly just as if she'd given birth to him.

And Carly snuggled up to him.

Piran liked watching them together. He liked seeing Carly cuddle the child in her arms while she gave him his bottle. He liked watching her bend over the baby while she changed him and dressed him. He liked the silly noises she made and the nonsense she talked, and he was amazed at the noises Arthur made in return. It was as if they were really communicating.

He looked down at the baby in his arms, then got up and carried him over to the sofa and set him in the corner, banked on either side by blue and green pillows.

Arthur regarded the pillows and Piran with equal curiosity.

'Are you going to yell?' Piran asked him nervously.

'Ba,' Arthur said. He patted a pillow.

Piran's eyes lit up. 'That's right,' he said. 'It's blue. And that one's green. Can you say green?'

'Ba ga,' said Arthur. He grabbed a pillow and stuffed the corner of it in his mouth, gumming it furiously.

'You're a genius,' Piran told him. 'You can say blue and green. My God! Carly!' he shouted. Then he remembered that Carly wasn't here.

He was alone. With a genius.

He gulped. He picked Arthur up again. 'Come on,' he said. 'Let's see what else you can say.'

He carried the baby all around the house, pointing out lamps and sofas, books and chairs. He took him outside and showed him palm trees and frangipani trees, breadfruit trees and bougainvillaeas.

'You might want to consider botany as a career,' he told Arthur. 'If you don't go into archaeology. I won't mind if you don't,' he assured the baby.

'Ga,' said Arthur. 'Da.'

Piran's eyes bugged. He held Arthur out at arm's length. 'Say that again,' he demanded. 'By George, kiddo, I think you just said Daddy!'

Carly started listening as soon as she came around the bend in the path, keeping her ears open for sounds of babies yelling. One particular baby at least.

She heard only the surf and the birds and a frog next to the mangrove tree.

She shifted the grocery bag from one arm to the other and climbed the steps to the deck. The vertical blinds were slanted to keep the afternoon sun out. The doors were open, but the screens were shut. Carly slid one open and looked around.

No Arthur. No Piran.

'Piran?' she said softly.

She got no response.

She frowned. If Arthur had gone to sleep, surely Piran would be working? If he had taken Arthur to the beach, she certainly would have seen them. She'd come back along the water and they weren't down there.

She carried the milk into the kitchen and put it in the fridge, then went in search of them.

They weren't on the veranda. They weren't in the small garden that faced the narrow drive. They weren't in Arthur's room either.

But they had been there. Carly saw a wet diaper on the floor. The romper she'd put Arthur in this morning was on the dresser. Several other T-shirts and rompers had been tossed aside.

Carly winced, wondering if Piran had taken Arthur and gone in search of someone who could help take care of him. She crossed the living room and pushed open the half-closed door to Piran's room.

And she smiled.

Piran, wearing only a pair of cut-off jeans, was sprawled flat on his back sound asleep on the bed. Arthur, clad in a diaper and a T-shirt, his knees drawn up under him and his thumb in his mouth, slept equally soundly on Piran's bare chest, one of his father's big hands cupped protectively around his back.

# CHAPTER SEVEN

'WHAT on earth is that?' Piran demanded as she came up the path. He had apparently awakened after she'd left to go back for the rest of her bounty, and now he was standing on the veranda staring down at her muzzily.

'It's a tree,' Carly panted.

'What are you dragging a tree around for?'

'Christmas.'

Piran blinked. '*What*?'

''Tis the season to be jolly. I'd forgotten.' She didn't say she'd been trying to forget. 'But when I went into town it became obvious and, well, I thought we ought to celebrate so I brought us a Christmas tree.' The explanation took every available bit of breath she had. She stopped and sagged against the railing at the bottom of the steps, fanning herself.

Piran looked at her as if she'd lost her mind. 'It looks like something you'd throw on a brush heap.'

'Well, there wasn't a lot of choice,' Carly said. 'Most of the pines I saw that looked sort of traditionally Christmassy were far too big. I thought about a banana tree because it came equipped with built-in ornaments——' she grinned '—but I didn't want to be the cause of the destruction of lots of little unripened bananas.'

He shook his head. 'What are you talking about?'

'Ben says that everyone who wants to just cuts a tree from the ones that grow near the beach. He told me where, so I walked back that way. Fortunately I found this one not far from the path up to the house.'

'And you just...cut it down?'

'Ben lent me a machete and——'

'What happened to the milk?' Piran demanded. 'You went to town to get milk.'

'I did, and I put it in the fridge. I bought some other things, too. Christmas presents. For Arthur.'

'You went Christmas shopping?' Piran gaped at her. 'You left me all morning and went Christmas shopping?'

'Yes, I did,' Carly said firmly. 'There's only eight more shopping days, you know. Besides, you did fine without me. You were both sleeping when I came in with the milk.'

He looked momentarily discomfitted. 'Luck,' he muttered. 'Anyway, don't you think we have enough to do with Arthur and the book without worrying about Christmas?'

'No, I don't. I think it's the most important thing we can do.'

'More important than the book?' he challenged her.

'Yes. Look,' she said with all the earnestness she could muster. 'I know it's due in barely more than two weeks. I know we've got a long way to go. And I know you're going to tell me Arthur won't remember.'

He opened his mouth to comment, but Carly went right on without letting him say a word.

'You're right, of course. He won't remember actual presents, actual events. But he'll sense it, I know he will. And it will matter, Piran. And later, when he's big enough to know and to ask, he will ask. He'll want to know about what happened when you first got him. He'll ask about *when* it happened. And you'll have to tell him it was near Christmas. And he'll want to know about his first Christmas. He'll want to know how you celebrated it. And you'll have to tell him that, too.

'So what are you going to tell him, Piran? That you were too busy writing your book to bother about it? That his first Christmas didn't matter? That it came and went and was no more than an annoyance? I don't think you want to do that. I think you want to be able to talk to him about the joy of the day, the joy of celebration. It was, after all, because of the arrival of a baby that we're celebrating Christmas at all!' Carly stopped, out of breath at last, and looked at him beseechingly.

Piran just stared at her. Then slowly he shook his head. 'My God, you're wasted on editing. Have you ever considered a career in law? You'd make a dynamite prosecuting attorney. Such incredible rhetorical talent going to waste...'

Carly felt her cheeks warm. 'Don't be obnoxious.'

'I'm not. I'm in awe.'

'You're laughing at me.'

He shook his head. 'I'm not laughing. There's damned little to laugh at right now, and you know it.'

She wasn't sure how broadly to interpret that comment so she steered away from it altogether. Their whole relationship was so complex that there had been little to laugh at since the beginning. Arthur only complicated it.

Or maybe, Carly thought, he simplified it. Maybe he made what was really important clear at last.

'I want Christmas,' Carly said, looking straight into Piran's deep blue eyes.

'And whatever Carly wants Carly gets?'

She was glad her gaze didn't falter. 'I think you already know the answer to that.'

He had the grace to wince a little.

'Never mind. It's all in the past,' Carly said. 'It's not important now.' She changed the subject briskly. 'Did Arthur give you a hard time?' She remembered the clothing scattered around the bedroom, remembered the sight of Piran on the bed with the baby asleep on his chest.

'He made his wishes known,' Piran said drily after a moment. 'And I wasn't always good at deciphering them.'

'I saw the clothes.' She slanted him a glance. 'Don't tell me he already has preferences in what to wear.'

A faint smile touched Piran's face. 'No. It turned out I did. Half of them I couldn't seem to get on him before he wiggled away from me. Finally I opted for the easiest route.'

'But you survived.'

'We survived. Did you know he can talk?'

'Piran, he's six months old!'

'Yeah, but he can say blue and green and good. At least I think he said good, and once he even said Daddy.'

'Daddy?'

He shrugged, embarrassed. 'Well, he doesn't enunciate very well yet, but what else could it have been?'

Carly shook her head. 'I can't imagine. Does this mean you're accepting the fact that you are his daddy?'

'Yeah, I guess I am,' he said. 'At least until another daddy comes along.'

It was a step. A small one, but still a step. They were bonding, Piran and Arthur. They had plenty more steps to take, of course, but they were finally on their way to becoming a family. Carly smiled. But it was a bittersweet smile because, heaven help her, she wanted to be part of the bond as well.

So she was a fool. So what else was new?

She was as incurable a romantic as her mother, as determined a believer in happy endings or at least in wonderful memories as the woman who'd given her life.

'Better to live and to love than to regret,' Sue had said to her daughter time and time again.

And while Carly could never see herself like Sue, trying to live and love seven different men, apparently she couldn't seem to stop trying to live and love with one— even if he didn't love her. Even if living with him meant only for the next two weeks and loving him meant only helping him learn to become a father and then walking away because that was the way he wanted it—just him and his child alone.

And for herself?

For herself Carly would take memories. They hurt sometimes—thinking about that joyous last Christmas which she'd spent with her mother and Roland and his daughters in Colorado still hurt. But hurting, Carly began to realize, was better than an empty life; it was better by far than feeling nothing at all.

So she dug in to make this Christmas a Christmas to remember.

She started with the tree.

Granted it wasn't beautiful, and Piran didn't seem to see its potential as he took it out of her hands and dragged it up the stairs for her. But maybe he would when they got it set up and began to decorate it. Carly dared to hope.

'Where do you want it?' he asked her when he'd lugged it up on to the deck.

'Er, perhaps in the living room in front of the window? I don't know. I mean, it's your house.'

'Nice of you to realize that,' he said drily. He carried the tree in and hoisted it upright and held it there. 'I don't suppose you bought a stand?'

'Oh, dear,' Carly said. She ran a nervous tongue over her lips and gave him a smile that was at least half sheepish grimace. 'I hadn't thought. Just—er—prop it

in the corner. I'll walk back to town and see if I can find
a tree stand at the hardware store.'

'Not on your life. We've got a book to do.'

'But the tree! I'm not going to abandon it, Piran!'
she said stubbornly.

'Obviously.'

'Well, then...'

He raked a hand through his hair. 'Don't worry. I'll
think of something.'

'You will?' She looked at him hopefully.

'I will. I promise,' he added when she gave him a look
that said she wasn't entirely convinced. 'Now, for the
ten thousandth time, we have to get going on the
book. I didn't get a single thing done this morning——'

'And you look far better for it. More rested. And you
probably feel better too, don't you, having spent some
time with Arthur?'

He scowled. 'What is this? Dr O'Reilly's shrink shop?'

Carly smiled slightly. 'Yes. And now Dr O'Reilly says
we need to decorate the Christmas tree.'

'Yeah? Well, first Dr St Just says you'd better work
on chapter seven.'

'But——'

'I mean it.'

Carly knew better than to push him further. She let
him think about it. But she wasn't above putting on a
tape of holiday music that she'd bought in town on the
stereo.

'Subliminal persuasion?' Piran arched a brow at her
when the first notes of 'Joy to the World' reached his
ears.

Carly smiled.

Piran studied her silently. 'It really means a lot to you?'

'Yes,' she said simply. 'It does.'

When Arthur woke up, Piran still hadn't done anything about the tree, but she thought he'd got the message. He was busy typing furiously so Carly went and got the baby. She brought him back out into the living room after she'd changed him. He looked happy and well-rested and none the worse for spending the morning with Piran.

He giggled as she danced him around the room to the tune of 'Frosty the Snowman'. Piran turned around to watch them. Carly waved Arthur's hand at him, then held it out in invitation.

'Want to dance with him?' she offered.

'I'll dance with you.'

'I already have a partner, thank you.'

'Frosty' ended and there was a moment's pause before the soft sound of 'What Child Is This?' began. Carly began to move with Arthur once more as Piran stood up and came toward them.

He took her hand, his grip firm and warm around her fingers. Then he wrapped his other arm around her back and, holding Arthur between them, he danced with her.

They moved slowly but smoothly with the music, looking into each other's eyes over the top of Arthur's head. The expression in Piran's gaze was warm and hungry and something more. Carly thought she saw a sort of puzzlement in them, as if he wasn't quite sure he had all the answers for a change.

They danced, and only when the last notes had long since died away did they stop at last.

Under the mistletoe.

Keeping his eyes on Carly's, Piran bent his head and kissed Arthur lightly on the top of his. Then he ran his tongue over still slightly parted lips.

'Kissing's not enough, Carlota,' he said, his voice ragged.

No, it's not, Carly wanted to say. But, fighting her own inclination as much as his because there was a limit to the amount of hurt she knew she could stand, she told him simply, 'It has to be.'

'For now,' he said.

The mail came very late that day, and Carly found herself holding her breath while Piran went to fetch it, though whether she hoped there was or wasn't a letter from Wendy she couldn't have said.

Only after Piran came back and all he had were two letters from colleagues, a postcard of a bathing beauty from Des in Fiji and a journal on Greek archaeology did she breathe again.

He tossed Carly the postcard as she sat giving Arthur a bottle and humming along to 'Silver Bells'. It was written in Des's almost illegible scrawl.

> Great so far. Meeting up with Jim and crew *mañana* for our sail into the great unknown. Be out of touch for a couple of weeks. Don't kill each other in the meantime—or me when I get back! Have a merry, merry one with lots of jolly surprises. Love, Des.

'Jolly surprise, huh?' Carly said, smiling and looking down at the baby in her arms. 'Wouldn't Des be shocked?'

Arthur gazed up at her solemnly.

'You're a very nice surprise,' Carly told him softly, and bent her head to drop a kiss on his nose. His eyelids began to droop. In minutes he was sound asleep. But Carly made no move to go put him down in his bed. Instead she listened as the music softly wove its holiday spell and looked at the child in her arms, marveling at the beauty of new life.

There was an ache in her throat as she envied Piran this wonderful child and the future they would share. And the ache got even worse when she started envying Arthur his future with Piran.

A sudden sound made her look up and she saw Piran standing in the doorway to the kitchen, watching her. The look on his face was intense, brooding and disturbingly sensual. If the embers had been banked when they'd held Arthur between them after the dance, they burst into flame now.

'Is he asleep?' Piran asked.

Carly nodded.

'Then put him down.'

And come to me. She didn't have to hear him say the words. She could see them in his eyes, in his slightly parted lips, in the heightened color that ran along his cheekbones.

And if she did go to him, if she did make love with him, what would she have then?

Memories, she told herself. You'd have memories.

And it was almost enough. But not enough to cancel out what she would have as well—a broken heart.

'Not now,' she said.

The look he gave her was long and fierce and aching. And then he turned away.

She wanted him. He *knew* she wanted him—probably as badly as he wanted her.

And yet she said no. And no again.

Why?

For *marriage*? What did marriage matter so much? When she'd been eighteen and using it to barter, he'd seen her as simply following in her mother's footsteps. But now...?

He was supposed to be working. He couldn't keep his mind on the caravel. He was supposed to be writing. He couldn't even spell words.

Except one. Carly. He typed it on to the screen. He erased it. His fingers typed it again.

He was as obsessed with her as he had been nine years ago. Only now he didn't have the folly of youth on which to blame it. He was old enough to know better—and he didn't.

He wanted Carly O'Reilly.

But even more, he discovered, he wanted to *understand* Carly O'Reilly.

With the folly of youth, he was sure he had.

Now he was far less certain.

She didn't need a man for support the way her mother had. She had a job and he'd be the first to admit she was good at it. She didn't need a man for self-esteem. She had plenty on her own. Yet she seemed very willing to share herself—except in bed, that was.

She positively doted on Arthur.

A part of Piran had assumed that watching her play mother to Arthur would quell his interest. But he'd been wrong about that, too. If anything, that interest was heightened.

Heightened, hell! It was driving him up the wall.

He finally heard her put Arthur down to bed. He expected her to leave, go for a walk, avoid him. But instead she came back through the living room and went into the kitchen and started doing something with pots and pans. He could hear her in there, humming along with that Christmas tape she'd bought. He deleted her name again and tried once more to make sense out of his notes.

It wasn't long until the sweet smell of Christmas baking drifted out of the kitchen and filled every corner of the house. His mouth watered. His stomach growled. He tried to ignore them. It wasn't any easier than ignoring her.

He got up and followed his nose into the kitchen. Carly was bent over taking a sheet of cookies out of the oven. He shut his eyes and braced his hand against the doorjamb.

'More subliminal suggestion?' he asked when he opened them again.

She smiled faintly. 'I wasn't going to,' she confessed. 'I didn't think I wanted to be reminded . . .' Her voice trailed off.

'Reminded?'

'These are my mother's recipes. She made the same kind of cookies every Christmas no matter where we were. And some of the places, to be honest, were pretty crummy. But she believed in keeping Christmas, in "keeping hope", she called it.' Carly smiled, a wistful, tender smile that tugged at something deep inside Piran.

'Last Christmas when she was with Roland and his daughters,' Carly went on, 'it was definitely the Christmas she'd always been hoping for—a celebration of family and love and joy. I didn't think I wanted to be reminded this year. I didn't think I wanted to re-member what I'd lost.' She stopped and rubbed at the corner of her eye, then smiled again. 'I was wrong. I still hope, I guess. And I wanted to share it with Arthur. Maybe he'll have some memory of these smells and re-member the happiness of his first Christmas.' She cleared her throat. 'Sorry. I'm getting sappy. It's the season, I guess.'

Piran just looked at her. She shifted uncomfortably under his gaze. 'Forget it. You can have one when they're cool. You might not have liked my mother, Piran, but she did make good cookies.'

'She did,' he said quietly. Then he said, 'I'm going for a walk.'

'It's hot out there. You'll die,' Carly warned.

Possibly. But he would definitely die in here if he didn't give in to the urge to go to her, to take her in his arms and hold her, to kiss her gently, to love her tenderly, and then to start all over again, replacing tenderness with passion, until both of them were sated with these feelings that had been growing between them for years.

He walked the length of the pink sand beach. He tried to cool his ardor, to get his perspective, to remind himself that the last thing he needed right now was a roll in a bed or on the sand or anyplace else with Carly O'Reilly. It would only complicate his already far too complicated life.

It worked only until he came around the point and saw her paddling in the shallows with Arthur in her arms. Then all his perspective vanished, all his ardor returned, and his preoccupation with Carly O'Reilly grew greater.

Carly saw him and waved Arthur's hand and her own.

Piran lifted a hand in reply. He didn't say anything, even as he came closer, and she gave him another smile.

'The cookies are cool now.'

'I'm not,' he said gruffly.

Her cheeks turned red. 'Piran, I——'

'Not your fault,' he muttered, and plunged past her into the surf. And the moment his head broke the surface he started stroking out to sea.

'Where are you going?' Carly called after him.

He didn't answer, just swam on.

Not until he reached the outer reef did Piran stop swimming and turn around, treading water and looking back at the woman and child on the shore. Carly was watching him. She was too far away for him to see the expression on her face, but the intensity of her gaze told him she was worried.

About him?

Did she think he was going to drown? Get eaten by a barracuda?

Did she care?

Yes, she probably did.

He'd seen enough of Carly over the past few weeks to know that she wasn't quite the manipulator he'd thought she was. No matter what he thought of her mother's marriage to his father, Carly clearly believed it had been for love. She'd been there for them both during his father's last illness. He hadn't. Stubborn and righteous to the last, he hadn't come even come to the old man's funeral.

God, what a bull-headed, moralistic prig he'd been.

He'd done his share of moralizing at Des, too, for all the good it had ever done, trying to get him to take their explorations seriously, to spend his time working and writing instead of sailing and partying.

Probably, he thought grimly, that was why Des had taken off for Fiji and left him alone with the book.

But Des hadn't left him totally alone; he'd sent him Carly.

Everything ultimately came back to Carly.

He looked at her now, never taking her eyes off him, as if he might vanish if she did. As if it were her responsibility to keep him safe. She held Arthur. His responsibility. She'd worked on the book for weeks. His book. She'd given up her holiday and taken over for Des who had left her to do his work.

When, Piran wondered, had anyone ever done anything for her?

*    *    *

Arthur squirmed in her arms when he saw Piran approach and Carly almost dropped him, so slick was he from having sunscreen rubbed all over his small body.

'Careful there,' Carly warned him. 'Hold still.'

'Give him to me.'

She looked round, startled to see Piran standing barely five feet from her. He held out his arms for Arthur.

She hesitated. 'You're volunteering?'

Taking the baby bodily out of her embrace seemed to be all the answer he was going to give her. But since Carly had no desire to get into a tug-of-war over the baby she let go and stepped back, feeling almost naked to his gaze as she did so.

But Piran's gaze didn't travel seductively down her body the way it often did. 'You go for a swim,' he suggested. 'Arthur and I will watch.'

Carly stared at him, uncertain how to take this turn of events. 'Fatherhood taking hold, is it?' she joked.

'Maybe.'

'Well, good. I really shouldn't swim, though. If you're going to take him, I'll just go back and get some work done.' She turned and started toward the beach.

'No, don't!'

At the urgency of his tone, Carly turned and looked at him again.

'Stay,' he entreated her.

It was a command, and yet it wasn't—quite. Carly looked back over her shoulder at him.

One corner of his mouth lifted in a wry smile. 'Arthur will think you're abandoning him if you go. He'll want to watch you.'

'Or you will?' she challenged him.

His lips pressed together for a moment. 'I can't help it,' he said eventually. He seemed almost unhappy about it. Probably he was, Carly thought. He'd never wanted to want her the way he did.

'I'll go for a quick swim,' she said. 'But then I really have to go back and finish what I was working on before Arthur woke up. I finished the cookies,' she said awkwardly. 'I didn't take all afternoon on them.'

'It doesn't matter. You deserve the break.'

'Well, it was nice. I'm glad I took it. But now I'm working on the part about the discovery and dating of the artifacts. It's going really fast. You're getting better,' she told him.

Piran grunted.

'Really,' Carly said, seeing the doubt on his face. 'Once you got into that it became almost like reading a detective novel.'

He nodded. 'It was almost like living a detective novel when we were doing it. When Des and I brought up that old gun like the ones they were making in Holland at the time, we had to try to figure out what circumstances existed that made the owners of a Spanish caravel buy Dutch guns...' He grinned self-consciously. 'Sorry. I'm babbling.'

Carly shook her head. 'No, you're not. I'm interested. Truly. I wish...' she began, then stopped abruptly.

'You wish what?'

'Nothing.' She turned away and started out into the water. 'Never mind. I'll swim.' She headed out toward the breakers.

Piran came with her.

'Piran! Arthur will be scared!'

'No, he won't. Will you?' he asked the baby, keeping pace with her. The water was almost to her breasts now. Bigger waves were coming in. Arthur's eyes were like dishpans, they were so huge. He gripped Piran's shoulders, but he didn't make a sound.

'You wish what, Carly?' Piran persisted.

Carly shrugged, letting her body rise with the lift of the wave. 'It's...not important. Just silliness.' She started to turn away. Piran's hand reached out and caught her arm.

'Tell me.'

She shrugged irritably. 'I was only going to say that I wish I had been able to go on a dive like that. There. See? No big deal.'

'An archaeological dive, you mean?'

'Any dive. I never have—except in the pool in New York. I——' she hesitated, then figured she might as well admit it '—took a course in scuba while I was helping Sloan with your last book. I thought it would give some insight into the process, the feeling, you know?'

'I'll take you.'

'Don't be ridiculous. The caravel is miles from here! Besides, we don't have any time. We don't have——'

'Not the caravel. Just out near the point at the top of the island in the narrows.' He pointed north. 'There's a wreck there—a Revolutionary War ship. Not a major discovery. Everyone has always known it was there, and it's been salvaged. But if it's your first time...just to give you a taste. You are certified?'

'Yes, but——'

'Fine. How about it?'

'We don't have time, remember?'

'We'll make time.'

'Arthur——'

'We can get an Arthur-sitter from somewhere. I'll ask Ruth and see if she knows someone.'

'It's silly.'

'No, it isn't. It's something you want to do.'

'And since when has that mattered to you?'

He winced. 'It matters,' he said. 'Besides, you're right. It might make you a better editor.'

'I doubt——'

'Come on, Carly. One lousy morning. We can go tomorrow.'

'I don't——'

'Chicken?'

'I am not chicken!' Her face flamed.

He grinned. 'Prove it. You must have wanted to pretty bad to get certified. Look me in the eye and say you don't want to do it, Carlota.' Deep blue eyes fastened on hers, challenging her, daring her to lie.

Carly sighed and positioned herself to try to catch the next wave. 'If you can get a sitter,' she muttered finally, secure in the knowledge that with the holiday coming he wouldn't be able to.

He did.

'Ruth's cousin, Mirabelle,' he told her that night after Ruth brought them supper. 'She'll keep Arthur while we're gone. We can drop him off first thing in the morning.'

'Drop him off?'

'Why not? He'll be fine,' Piran assured her. 'If he can cope with being dropped off on us, he'll be able to handle a morning at Mirabelle's.'

Carly was sure that he was right, but it still made her nervous. She was feeling more and more as if Arthur was her responsibility and less and less as if she wanted to entrust him to anyone else.

'She is qualified, isn't she?' she asked Piran.

'If having six of your own qualifies you,' he answered with a grin.

So Carly had to be satisfied with that.

If she could have, she'd have said she'd changed her mind. It was crazy going diving with Piran. It wouldn't serve any purpose at all—except to make her more aware than ever of what life would have been like if he'd loved her and married her years ago.

She didn't want to know, damn it!

And yet she did.

Heaven help her, she wanted to spend the morning diving with Piran. She would have nothing else. She wouldn't make love with him. She didn't want those memories. They'd hurt too much.

But memories of diving, of sharing their experience underwater, of fulfilling one of her dreams—yes, those she could handle. At least, she would try to.

She was in such a turmoil thinking about that and trying instead to think about the chapter she was supposed to be editing once Arthur went to sleep that she wasn't really paying much attention to what Piran was up to.

It was a shock, therefore, to hear a thud on the deck and to look out to see him wrestling a good sized bucket up the steps.

'What are you doing?'

'Putting up your Christmas tree.' He hoisted the bucket again and carried it into the house. He set it in front of the window, fetched the tree and planted it in the bucket which was, she saw, filled a third of the way up with sand. 'Come here and hold this while I finish shoring it up.'

Bemused, Carly did as she was told, holding the tree, marveling not simply at Piran's resourcefulness, but at the fact that he'd actually bothered.

Now he came back to kneel next to the tree and put rocks around it inside the bucket, wedging it tightly, then filling the rest of the bucket with sand.

As he worked, Carly watched the ripple of the muscles in his back. He was so close that his dark hair brushed against her bare legs. She stepped away. But she couldn't go far without letting go of the tree and she didn't dare do that. Piran finished with the rocks and the sand.

He straightened and said, 'Hold out your hand.'

Carly looked at him warily, but he didn't say anything, just waited, and she finally did what he said.

He reached in his pocket and placed two pieces of sea glass—one red, one blue—into her palm. 'I found them when I was picking up rocks,' he told her. A corner of his mouth twisted. 'I—uh—remembered you liked the one we found a long time ago. I... thought you might like these.'

Carly blinked, then swallowed. 'Thank you.' Her fingers closed on them. They looked at each other for a long moment—there were so many messages in that look. So many confusing feelings.

'Now water,' Piran decreed abruptly, and got to his feet once more to go and fetch some.

Carly watched him go, her fingers tight around the smooth pieces of glass. She had told herself for years that all her fascination with Piran had been one-sided, that she had built everything up in her head, that no one else would remember all the details she remembered.

How had Piran remembered about the sea glass?

He came back with a bucket full of water, then added more sand as the water packed it more densely. 'There,' he said at last, nodding his approval. 'That ought to hold it. What do you think?'

'It's wonderful,' she said, then looked away, still feeling dazed. Her eyes flickered back to him briefly. 'Thanks.'

'Did you buy lights?'

'What? Oh—er—yes. Of course.' She managed to get her brain functioning again, went to where she had left the bag on the counter in the kitchen and take out the three strings of colored lights.

She held them out to Piran. He shook his head. 'I did my part. You can decorate.' He paused for a split second after he said it, making her wonder if she could have argued with him. But, before she could make up her mind, abruptly he turned away and went back to the keyboard.

For a long moment Carly stood with the lights in her hands, looking at the back of Piran's dark head and the hunch of his broad shoulders. She felt such a crazy mix of emotions that she didn't think she would ever sort them out.

He felt only lust for her, she told herself. Lust and passion. He wanted sex. And a good editing job. And someone to care for Arthur.

But he had remembered the sea glass.

And he had offered to take her diving in the morning. He had taken the time to find a way to put the tree up tonight.

God, she had to stop thinking like this! It was useless. Worse than useless.

But where Piran was concerned she was like a moth with a flame, attracted, mesmerized. Yet she knew full well what would befall her if she gave in to her fascination with him and dared too much, ventured too close.

She put the lights on the tree alone. She went to bed without saying goodnight. She tossed and turned for hours.

Piran went to bed shortly after midnight. She heard him get up an hour or so later, prowl around the house, then let himself out to go down to the beach.

She was still awake at past two when he came back and came to stand just outside her door. She lay unmoving, every nerve alert and aware.

Wanting. Hoping? Fearing.

Then she heard his footsteps as he walked into his own room and the sound of the springs as he fell into his bed once more.

She should be glad, she told herself. She should be rejoicing that he respected her boundaries.

She did. Of course she did.

It was perverse, then, that, having got what she wanted, she felt even worse.

# CHAPTER EIGHT

MIRABELLE thought Arthur was the most beautiful child she had ever seen. She clucked and fussed over him, bouncing him on her hip and tickling his tummy. She got belly laughs out of him that Carly had never thought were in there. And then she shooed Piran and Carly on their way.

'You don't be worryin' about him now. He be fine. Won't you, mon?' she asked a still giggling Arthur. He grinned and waved his arms.

'I think he likes her,' Carly grumbled to Piran as they left and walked down to the dock.

'That's bad?' He slanted her a sidelong glance.

'I suppose not,' she said, but she still felt unaccountably irritated.

Piran grinned. 'Just a little jealous, maybe?'

Carly scowled at him.

His grin widened. 'Relax. He'll be fine, just like she said. Come on.' He grabbed her hand and hauled her with him down the hill. 'Stop thinking about Arthur and think about what a good time you're going to have fulfilling your heart's desire.'

How could he have known? Carly wondered an hour later as she swam lazily alongside him, heading down to the wreck of the old ship that she could see in the crystalline depths.

Maybe he didn't, she conceded. But he was right.

Ever since she'd known the St Justs, ever since she had been so briefly and disastrously a part of their lives, she'd dreamed about a day like this one—a day when she would dive with Piran, swim with him, share with him the joy of his profession.

She turned her head to see him swimming half a length ahead of her. His dark hair was streaming back except where it was pressed against his head by the rubber strap of the mask he wore. He was pointing at something and she looked where he was indicating to see a school of shimmering, almost iridescent blue fish.

Everywhere she looked, life abounded. When you were in a boat or even simply wading, you never saw all the things that lived around you just below the surface. Not only the fish, but the corals, the sponges, the huge array of kelps and anemones. At least, that was what she thought they were. When she got back to the city, she would have to take a class, have to learn what all these amazing things were that she was seeing now firsthand.

Piran beckoned to her, then swam down closer to the wreck. It was encrusted with years and years of coral, and of course all the significant archaeological artifacts had long since been removed. There wasn't the thrill of discovery that Carly knew must come from the excavation and careful salvage of a newly discovered wreck. But still there was excitement.

There was the wonder she felt at seeing the boat right where it had gone down, still a part of the natural world, not merely an exhibit in a museum. There was a flicker of astonishment that the boat was so small. When she thought of ships, she thought of the *QE II* or the *Queen Mary*. It was probably an optical illusion, but she thought the lifeboats on the *QE II* were probably as big as this entire ship was.

And most of all there was Piran.

She was sure that a dive to show her a wreck like this one must be tedious to a man like him. But if it was he gave no sign. On the contrary, he seemed almost eager.

He moved ahead, pointing to things, explaining by hand signals as best he could what they had once been.

Twice he caught her hand and tugged her close so that he could point out something small that she might have missed otherwise. If she could have, with the breathing apparatus in her mouth, Carly would have been smiling all over her face. As it was, she simply followed him eagerly, taking it all in, relishing every moment. She didn't want to leave, even when Piran indicated that their tanks were running low on air.

It wasn't until they were back in the boat that she actually thought again about Arthur. Even then she only thought of him fleetingly, long enough to hope that he was still enjoying his morning at Mirabelle's, before her attention was captured once more by the man she had been diving with.

Piran was taking off his gear while Ben helped her with hers. She stumbled as the boat rocked and it was Piran who caught her before she fell. He righted her, but didn't let go.

'You OK?'

'F-fine,' Carly assured him. She turned, her eyes sparkling. 'Wonderful.' She had to say it, had to let him know how much the dive had meant to her. 'It was fantastic.'

He grinned. 'Yes. It was.'

'You was down there long enough,' Ben grumbled. 'Didn't catch nothing up here.'

'Sorry,' Piran said lightly as he tugged her down and sat beside her.

But Carly didn't think he sounded as if he regretted it. He looked as if he'd enjoyed it as much as she had, though of course that was impossible. Still, it made her feel almost light-headedly happy as Ben piloted them back toward the harbor.

'Tell me all about what we were seeing down there,' she said to him. 'You were pointing out some stuff, but I didn't know what it was.'

He began to explain. Carly listened intently, absorbing it all. When she didn't understand, she asked more. Perhaps she was making a fool of herself, betraying her ignorance. But she really wanted to know. She wanted to know everything he did.

And as she listened she lifted her face into the balmy tropical breeze, letting it caress her damp skin. The December sun warmed her gently. Piran's hard, hair-roughened thigh pressed against her own with a heat far more intense. She knew she should move away.

But this was fantasy. Make-believe. The stuff of which dreams and memories were made. As long as she knew it wasn't real, wasn't going anywhere, she could enjoy it.

Couldn't she?

Their diving expedition had started as a way to do something for her. It had become more than that almost at once and he'd been doing it for himself as much as for her. She bewitched him.

Of course, he reminded himself as they walked back to pick up Arthur from Mirabelle's, she always had.

Her long legs and lithe figure and saucy smile had intrigued him since the moment he'd laid eyes on her. But other things about her attracted him as well.

The way she handled Arthur, of course. And the way she'd dug in and helped him make something of the book Des had left him with. And her desire to make this Christmas special. But now, this morning, it was her fascination with diving that bewitched him.

He'd taken plenty of starry-eyed women diving. He'd known what to expect. To a woman, they'd shown cursory interest in the wreck and a whole lot more interest in the tangling of limbs with him underwater.

Not Carly. Carly had been all business. She'd followed him intently, but unless he'd touched her to point something out she'd kept her distance.

Still, her interest in what he'd shown her had been genuine. After they'd come up, she'd plied him with questions that she'd really seemed to want to know the answers to. Piran never liked talking about diving or archaeology when he felt he could be boring his listeners. He didn't feel he bored Carly.

'There's a train underwater near here,' he told her as they turned the corner on to Mirabelle's street. 'You should see it. You'd like it.'

'I'd like anything,' Carly agreed, her eyes shining.

I'll take you, Piran almost said. We'll make a day of it. You and me.

But he didn't say it. Because they didn't have time. There was no way they could go to see the train. Carly had been right when she'd said they really hadn't had time for this dive. But he wanted to.

He wanted to share it with her, to show her, to see her eyes light up the way they'd lit up today.

So they'd lost a morning on the book. He was glad. It had been good for both of them.

And after the book was done? he asked himself.

After the book was done, well, she'd go back to New York, and he'd take off for Greece to his next project.

Chances were he'd never see Carly O'Reilly again.

The thought gave him a curiously hollow feeling.

They were almost at Mirabelle's gate when Piran knew he had to say the one thing he'd never thought he would say.

'Remember . . . your birthday nine years ago?'

Carly's head jerked round and she stared at him, the expression in her eyes like that of a doe caught in a hunter's sight. He saw her swallow.

'What about it?'

Now that he'd brought it up, he wasn't sure where to start. He ducked his head briefly, then lifted it again to meet her gaze. 'I was a jerk. What I said...what I thought.' He paused, then continued grimly, 'I was a jerk when you got here, thinking the same thing.'

Carly didn't say anything. Her eyes were as round as old Spanish doubloons.

'I don't know what excuse I can give you,' he said gruffly, aware of the hot blood in his cheeks. 'That I was young and stupid and full of myself? That I didn't trust women? Any women? Even young naïve ones? Hell, I don't know. Take your pick.'

He saw Carly wince when he said the bit about young naïve ones.

She licked her lips before she spoke. 'Yes, well, I'm sure that my mother marrying your father must have been a terrible shock,' she began slowly.

He nodded. 'It's just that she was just so bloody different from him—from us! I know my folks didn't get along, I know my mother left my father for another man. But I never figured my dad would go for...for...'

'Someone like my mother?' Carly suggested drily, with only the faintest hint of hurt in her voice.

Piran shifted uncomfortably. 'Someone so different,' he said. 'My mother was so quiet and remote and...and elegant, despite what she did.' He grimaced. 'I guess I thought that was what my father liked. But then he met yours and she was...she was...'

'Flamboyant?' Carly suggested wryly. 'Jolly? Devil-may-care?'

'I wasn't used to it. It made me suspicious. I . . . think she made my dad happy, though,' he admitted after a moment, rubbing a hand through his salt-stiffened hair. 'She must have.' He stared off into the distance, remembering, then he swallowed against the suddenly tight feeling in his throat. 'He chose her.'

'Over you, you mean?' Carly said.

Piran pressed his lips together. It sounded so rotten put that way, but she was right. 'I shouldn't have pushed him to forget her,' he said. 'I shouldn't have walked out when he wouldn't.'

'You did what you thought was right,' Carly said. 'But you should have come back . . . at the end.'

He bowed his head. 'I know.' He lifted his gaze and met hers. 'I'm sorry I didn't.'

'He knew you loved him,' Carly said. 'And he loved you. He told me so.'

Piran ran his tongue across dry lips. 'I'm glad.'

'My mother loved him, you know,' Carly said, and he heard a catch in her throat. 'She really did.'

Yes, she probably had, Piran realized now. He looked at the ground between his feet. He didn't know what he expected. Absolution, maybe? A blessing from the young woman he'd disbelieved all those years ago, from the woman he'd been rude to just days before?

Fat chance. Whatever words he was waiting for never came. Carly didn't move to go through the gate, but she didn't speak either. She simply stood there, and finally Piran flicked a sidelong glance in her direction.

'He deserved being loved,' Piran said softly. 'He was a good man.' A better man than I'll ever be, he added silently.

'Everyone deserves to be loved,' Carly said softly.

Their eyes met. Hers were wide and caring and seemed to offer him her heart. The same way she'd offered it to him nine years ago.

He shut his eyes against the memory of the innocent child she had been.

'Well,' she said more briskly after a moment, 'thank you for taking me diving today. I enjoyed it.'

Once more he thought about offering to take her to see the train.

And then he knew he'd better leave well enough alone.

The next afternoon there was a pastel envelope in the post. Carly picked it out of the basket with a quiver of apprehension, studied it for a moment, then carried it in and dropped it on the keyboard on top of Piran's fingers.

They closed around it. His knuckles went almost white.

'It's postmarked over two weeks ago,' Carly said.

Piran reached for the letter-opener and slit it open and began to read.

Carly bit her lip, resisting the temptation to step round behind him and read it over his shoulder.

It wasn't long. In mere seconds she saw his teeth come together. He leaned his head back against the chair and shut his eyes. He swallowed. Then he opened his eyes, folded the letter carefully once more and stuck it back in the envelope.

'Well, I guess that's it,' he said flatly.

'What'd she say?'

'That she has a surprise for me. She says she's sure I'll be thrilled. At least——' he lifted his gaze and met Carly's again '—she hopes I will be.'

'A surprise,' Carly echoed hollowly, and felt sick.

She didn't know what she'd expected the letter to say. She supposed maybe she'd been hoping it would say, In case you find a baby on your veranda someday, it isn't mine.

Piran's lips pressed together in a flat line. 'Must've got lost in the mail for a while. It should've got here before Arthur came.'

'So I suppose that makes Wendy Arthur's mother,' Carly said in a voice as toneless as his.

What difference did it make? she asked herself. Someone had to be Arthur's mother. She knew she wasn't.

She just wished she were.

There. She'd admitted it. She'd put the thought into words, even though only she had heard them, acknowledged the truth of them.

Piran's apology yesterday had left her stunned. And aching. All the hopes, all the dreams, all the 'might have beens' wouldn't leave her alone. She hadn't been able to settle for the rest of the day. She'd done her best to look as if she was working. She'd felt a complete fraud.

She'd gone to bed early, hoping that tomorrow would be better, that she would have her equilibrium back. So far, it wasn't much of an improvement.

'Didn't she at least say why she was going to leave him with you?' she asked rather desperately.

'She didn't say much. Just some babble about her surprise making me take her seriously.'

'Well, it's certainly done that,' Carly said.

'Hasn't it just?'

They were silent for a long moment, each absorbed in his and her own thoughts.

Then, 'Damn!' Piran smacked his fist on the desktop. 'I wish to God I'd read those earlier letters!'

Before Carly had a chance to ask what good it would have done, Arthur, with a surprisingly well-developed sense of good timing, set up a wail from the bedroom.

Carly jumped out of her chair and hurried to pick him up.

'Swim time?' Piran asked when she came back after having changed and fetched him.

'Maybe I shouldn't take the time today,' Carly said.

'Why not?'

'I... haven't been getting a lot done. I've been... distracted.'

'You've been working flat out all day. We both have.'

'But we've only got a little more than a week and a half until it's due.'

'We'll make it. And do you honestly think we can work with him awake? Both of us?'

'Probably not,' Carly admitted. 'But one of us ought to.'

Piran nodded. 'Then I will.'

She was relieved that he wouldn't be coming with them. 'We won't be long,' she promised. 'Hold him, will you, while I change into my suit?'

She held out the baby and Piran showed no hesitation in taking him. He even dropped a kiss on Arthur's forehead.

Something in the area of Carly's heart suddenly seemed to squeeze tight. She hurried out the room and went in to her own, stripping off her shorts and shirt and pulling on her suit. Then she caught her hair up in a ponytail, slipped her feet into beach sandals and went back to get Arthur.

'Thanks.' She picked up two towels, scooped the baby out of Piran's arms and headed toward the door. 'See you in a while.'

'Yeah.'

She knew she'd promised not to take long, but once she got down to the beach where the water was warm, the breeze was gentle, and Arthur clearly loved it—it was far easier to stay than to go back and be with Piran.

Because she wanted to be with Piran, heaven help her, and the more she was with him, the more tangled her emotions became.

She wanted things to happen that she knew would never happen—love, marriage, family, happily ever after. She'd told herself she'd outgrown that nonsense where he was concerned. And she'd even half believed it until yesterday.

And then, when he'd apologized, when he'd told her he'd been wrong about her—and her mother—all those years ago, all her hopes had come flooding back.

God, she was such a fool.

'Ah, da!' Arthur jumped in her arms, a wide grin spreading across his face as he waved his hands.

'Glad to see me, are you?'

Carly spun round in the water, almost falling as she did so. Piran was close enough to reach out and catch her, pulling both her and Arthur against him.

'See?' he said to Carly. 'I told you he could talk!'

'What are you doing here?'

He gave her a guilty grin. 'I have no willpower?'

'Piran, really—you need to——'

'Relax. I finished the chapter and I decided to reward myself with a swim. OK?'

He was still holding them and Carly didn't think it was OK at all. And there was no way she was going to be able to relax. Her body was responding even to that much contact. She tried to wriggle away. 'So go swim,' she said gruffly.

'In a minute. I think a reward from you would be nice, too.'

'What kind of reward?' Carly said suspiciously.

'A kiss?'

Her eyes narrowed. 'I never gave you a kiss for finishing any of the others!'

'Obviously we need to renegotiate.'

She gave him a shove. 'Go swim.'

He feigned hurt, but he let her and Arthur go, turning to plunge under an incoming wave and swimming with long, powerful strokes out toward the reef. Carly stood and watched him, her body still tingling, her heart still hammering.

'Ah, da,' Arthur said again.

'Oh, yes,' Carly agreed. 'Oh, yes.'

Piran swam almost to the reef, then turned and swam parallel to the shore. Carly walked in the water, keeping abreast of him, her eye always on his dark head as it dipped and rose with the movement of the waves. At last he turned and started swimming back and she turned too and stayed with him.

'Someday you'll swim like that,' she told Arthur.

Arthur giggled and gummed her shoulder, then tugged on her ponytail and grabbed her ear. 'Uh, da!' he chortled.

Carly hugged his small, slippery body close, cherishing these moments, knowing how soon the time would come when she would be missing him.

And Piran.

They had reached the spot where the trail led back up the hill toward the house now and Piran was swimming back toward her. As he reached the shallows and emerged, the water slid down his strong muscled chest, plastered his navy boxer-style trunks against his abdomen, against his groin. He looked like Neptune, Carly thought, rising from the sea. He was looking right at her, his eyes dark, his mouth smiling.

And then he looked beyond her up toward the beach, and he stopped smiling. He hesitated, and she saw something flicker in his gaze. Then he came toward her more quickly and reached out to grasp her arm. He slipped his around her shoulder.

'What's the matter?' Carly said, because this touch was not quite the same as the earlier one. That one had been teasing and easy, albeit hungry. This one was pure leashed tension.

'Piran?' She slanted a glance at him, but he wasn't even looking at her.

His gaze was fixed on a woman who must have been standing at the bottom of the trail and was now coming across the beach. She had thick, honey-coloured hair that hung loose down her back. She wore white shorts and a flame-red halter-top. She was slightly curvier than the average model, but no less beautiful. She reminded Carly of exactly the sort of women who had swarmed around Piran all those years ago—the pretty, pouty ones who adored him and whom he had adored in turn.

'Piran!'

The woman was waving now, smiling broadly, and Piran muttered under his breath, 'Give me Arthur,' and promptly took him from Carly before she could even make a move. He strode doggedly out of the water holding the child, hauling Carly with him until he stopped to face the woman.

She wasn't smiling now. She looked apprehensive, confused as she looked from him to Arthur and Carly.

'Wendy,' Piran said curtly.

Carly's jaw dropped. *Wendy*?

This was Arthur's mother?

Wendy was regarding Piran nervously. 'You...got my letter?'

A corner of Piran's mouth lifted sardonically. 'Today.'

She blanched. 'Oh, dear. So you weren't expecting...' Her voice wavered and faded away.

'No, my dear, I certainly wasn't expecting...' Piran drawled, twisting the final word.

'So you're not...happy?'

'On the contrary,' Piran said, 'I'm quite happy, thank you very much.'

Wendy brightened. 'You are?'

'Yes. I'm also married.'

She stared at him. So did Carly.

'Married?' Wendy echoed.

*Married*? Carly thought just as he hauled her forward and said, 'This is my wife. Carlota. Carly, this is Wendy Jeffries. You remember me telling you about her.' His grip meant there was only one answer to that. He was going to leave bruises for days.

'O-of course. How nice to meet you,' she stammered.

Wendy didn't say anything. She just stared—first at Piran, then at Carly, and finally at Arthur.

'He's——' she started, but Piran cut her off.

'He's mine,' he said in a tone that brooked no argument. 'I'll admit it wherever it needs to be admitted. I'll take full responsibility in the courts, wherever I have to. I fully intend to provide for him; you don't have to worry.'

Wendy blinked. 'What?'

'I said, you don't have to worry about Arthur. Obviously you don't want him. Fair enough. I don't blame you in the circumstances. But Carly and I do want him.'

Wendy stared at him. So did Carly. Wendy opened her mouth, then closed it again. Then she ran her tongue over her lips as if she was considering what to say.

'Do you have a problem with that?' Piran demanded in a tone that said she'd better not have.

'Piran, I——'

'Look, I don't know all the legal ins and outs. I've never had a kid before, belie've me. Probably I owe you something—support, recompense, I don't know. Whatever it is, I'll do right by you as long as Carly and I can keep him.'

'Piran——'

'You can talk to my lawyer! We'll go back up to the house and I'll get you his number. I'll call him first and you can when you get back to the States. He'll straighten everything out, do the legal——'

'*Piran*!'

'What is it?'

'The baby—Arthur? He's...not mine.'

'*What*?' Piran yelled it. Carly thought it. They both stared at Wendy Jeffries. 'What did you say?'

Wendy shrugged helplessly. 'You seem to think that I...that we... Did someone leave you a baby?'

'Someone left me Arthur,' Piran said tersely. 'On the veranda a little over a week ago. I thought it was you! He's the right age, damn it. And you said...you wrote me all those letters! You wrote about a surprise!' He glared at her accusingly.

Wendy flushed deeply. 'I didn't mean...I was trying to reestablish what little relationship we'd begun. We didn't meet in the best of circumstances, as you might recall. It was a terrible time in your life.'

'I know. That's why I thought...'

'You were hurting badly. You talked about it a lot. To me. And then I didn't see you any more. But for one night we had been close. And I thought maybe it meant something. I hoped it meant something,' she admitted. 'I thought I'd see if things were better with you now. So I wrote. Lots. I was a fool, I guess. And I had some vacation coming and before Thanksgiving I saw Des and he said you were both going to be here over Christmas. So I thought I'd come down. He never said you were married!'

Piran's jaw set tight. The color on his face was at least as deep as it was on hers.

'Arthur couldn't be mine, Piran,' she said after a moment. 'We never even made love.'

Piran looked as if he wanted the ocean to come and swallow him up. He shook his head desperately. 'I couldn't—I didn't...remember it all. Like you said, I was a basket case back then. After Gordon died. I remember going back to your apartment and then——' he shrugged '—I don't remember what happened. When Arthur showed up, I just assumed——'

'No. You drank. You talked. You cried. And then you fell asleep in my bed,' Wendy told him. 'I thought we might have something eventually. As I said, I hoped. But we never made love.'

Piran bent his head. 'Oh, lord, I'm sorry,' he muttered. 'I never meant—— Oh, geez, what a mess.'

'I shouldn't have come,' Wendy said.

Piran grimaced wryly. 'Probably better that you did, though maybe not as far as you're concerned. But now at least I know you're not his mother.'

'But you don't know who is.'

He sighed. 'No.'

Wendy looked from Piran to Carly, then back at Piran again, and shook her head. 'You have an understanding wife, Piran. You're lucky. She really must love you.'

'It's not a bad idea, you know,' Piran said that evening after they had seen Wendy on to the water taxi and Ben had given them a ride back home.

They hadn't had a moment alone to discuss anything until Ben left, and once he had Arthur had needed feeding and while Carly had done that Piran had disappeared down to the beach.

Carly hadn't called him back. She hadn't known what to say to him. She still didn't. And she didn't really know what he was talking about now.

She looked up from the manuscript she'd been trying to concentrate on. He was standing just inside the door, staring out the window into the darkness, not looking at her, one hand tucked into the pocket of his shorts, the other balled lightly into a fist. 'What are you talking about?'

'Getting married.'

'Getting married?' The words gave her stomach an odd roller coaster feeling when she said them.

'I thought about it while I was walking and I thought, Why not?' He gave her a sidelong glance. 'I mean, it's what you wanted, isn't it? That's what you said.'

'I didn't mean——'

He raked his fingers through his hair. 'I know you didn't mean like this, but let's be logical. Why the hell shouldn't we? God knows we've wanted each other for years!'

'For heaven's sake, Piran——'

'We have. You can't deny it. And we would have made love by now if you'd been willing, and you know it. You haven't been because you want marriage. So, OK, I'm offering marriage.' He looked right at her as he said it.

Carly felt a pain where the roller coaster had been. 'Such a charming proposal,' she said with as much lightness as she could muster.

Piran kicked at the rug underfoot. 'I'm sorry. But you must know by now that romantic is not really my style. And this whole mess hasn't exactly been charming, you have to admit. But it would work,' he went on a little desperately. 'Surely you must see that?'

'There's more to marriage than wanting each other,' Carly said faintly, unsure exactly what she saw beyond a meshing of her wildest dream and her worst nightmare.

'We've got more. You like Arthur, don't you?'

'Of course I like Arthur!'

'And you like it here?' He looked at her for confirmation then went on. 'And you like to dive. You said you'd always wanted to dive. If we get married, you'll be able to dive all the time. Here. In Greece. Maybe in the Pacific if that business Des is looking into works out. And we're doing good together on the book, aren't we?'

'Yes,' Carly admitted, her throat tight.

'So, like I said, why not? We get married and Arthur has two parents. You get to dive. We can write books together all day and have sex together all night.' He looked positively pleased with himself.

Carly wanted to scream. 'What about Arthur's mother, whoever she is?'

'What about her?'

'When she shows up——'

'She can damned well leave again! She doesn't want him. She proved that. If she hasn't come by now, she hasn't got a chance in hell of getting him back from me. Especially if I'm married.' He looked at her now, his dark gaze intent. 'Come on, Carly. What do you say?'

Carly couldn't answer. Her tongue was glued to the roof of her mouth. Her mind spun. Her heart seemed to have stopped.

Marry Piran? Be Arthur's mother? Share their lives every day? Travel and dive and write books with Piran for years to come?

Just like that. It felt so right—and yet so wrong. So logical. So cold-blooded.

And yet Carly didn't feel cold-blooded at all. She yearned. She ached.

Piran didn't move. He waited.

'If I . . . if I say no?' Carly whispered after a moment. 'What then?'

He frowned. 'What do you mean, what then?'

'I mean, are you just going to go into town and ask the next woman you meet?'

'What do you think I am? I want you. It solves all our problems, doesn't it? You want marriage. I want a mother for Arthur. We both want to go to bed!' The smile he gave her had a wry, almost wistful quality to it. 'But if you say no I'm not just going to go looking for another warm body, I promise.'

As a marriage proposal, it left a lot to be desired. John's mere hinting had been considerably more romantic than Piran's flat suggestion. But Carly didn't want to marry John.

She'd never stopped wanting to marry Piran.

But, even acknowledging that, she hesitated to say yes. It seemed the height of folly to get into a marriage that was no more than a convenience.

But perhaps it was a bigger folly not to be willing to try.

She didn't believe that Piran would cheat on her. When he gave his word, he kept it. He tried to do the right thing. He was morally upright and judgmental almost to a fault. He also believed in duty. If he said marriage vows with her, Carly felt he would honor them.

Marriages had started with less.

She heard a whimper from the bedroom. And, of course, there was Arthur. She would have Piran. And she would have Arthur. Maybe she would have other children. A home. A family. Her childhood dreams come true.

Well, perhaps not quite.

But close.

She remembered her mother, leaping into marriage after marriage, always hoping for the best.

'You can't be afraid to risk, Carly,' she'd told her daughter time and time again, even when she'd got hurt.

Carly knew she could get hurt marrying Piran. But would she hurt less if she turned him down?

She looked at him, still waiting.

'All right,' she said slowly, lifting her gaze and meeting his levelly. 'I'll marry you. Yes.'

# CHAPTER NINE

THEY got engaged, they fed and changed Arthur and put him to bed, and then they finished chapter eight.

'I'll get started on nine,' Piran said when he'd approved her corrections. 'The last chapter. You look tired. You can go on to bed.' His tone was brusque, not exactly that of a doting fiancé.

Carly gave him a wan smile and nodded. 'Yes, I am tired. I'll see you in the morning,' she said.

But Piran was already consulting his notes and pecking away at the keyboard. He didn't even turn around.

She hadn't really expected romance, she thought as she stripped off her clothes and got ready for bed. After all, their 'engagement' was not precisely a love match. Not on Piran's side, at least. On her own, no matter how much she might wish otherwise, she very much feared that it was.

She didn't admit it, of course. The only thing she had left, it sometimes seemed, was the dignity she was clinging to by not wearing her heart on her sleeve.

If Piran knew how much she loved him, she wouldn't even have that.

She washed her face and brushed her teeth and stared at her reflection in the mirror. 'You are engaged to Piran St Just,' she told herself out loud.

Years ago she had said those words to herself in the mirror, trying them out, and they'd made her smile secretly and hug her feelings for him close against her heart.

Now the smile wouldn't come, and the feelings that hugged her heart were tangled with feelings of worry.

Would it work? Would they be good parents for Arthur? Good spouses to each other?

Would Piran ever really care about her?

'Tune in tomorrow,' she advised her reflection, 'for the next exciting installment of the "Follies of Carly O'Reilly".'

'And what follies would those be?' asked a voice from just beyond the half-opened door.

Carly spun around, her mouth sounding a faint, 'Oh!' She stepped back, bumping into the sink, surprised.

Piran gave her a wry grin. 'You were expecting someone else?'

Carly shook her head, flustered. 'Of course not. What do you want?'

'To kiss you goodnight?'

Carly's eyes widened. She groped for the towel and held it in front of her thin nightgown, realizing even as she did so how foolish she was being. She scraped her dignity together.

'Fine,' she said, and leaned forward quickly and just far enough to brush her lips along the line of his jaw, then pulled back. 'Goodnight.'

Piran shook his head slowly. 'Not good enough.'

Still clutching the towel, Carly tried to move past him, but he didn't budge. 'Don't be silly, Piran. I'm going to bed and you've got to get to work on chapter nine.'

'No, I don't.'

'But you said——'

'I know what I said. I was being noble. I wasn't going to push. But——' he shrugged ruefully '—I have a very low nobility span, it seems.'

He didn't say anything else, offered no more arguments, no convincing lines. He simply stood quietly, speaking and touching her only with his beautiful eyes.

Carly felt the heat of his gaze as if he'd made physical contact. A delicate frisson began at her shoulders and swept slowly down over her breasts, the curve of her hips, the tanned length of her legs. Everywhere Piran's eyes touched her, her body grew taut and seemed to hum with awareness.

'What follies, Carly?' he asked again, his voice barely more than a whisper. 'Follies like this?' He lifted his hand and touched her cheek, traced her jawline with one finger, then ran it along the line of her lips and finally leaned toward her to touch them with his own.

There was no demand in this kiss, no urgency, only a lazy, teasing playfulness, a hint, a promise. It was a nibble, no more.

'Was that a folly, Carly?' he asked softly. 'Is this?'

His lips met hers again. This kiss was longer. It touched, teased, tasted. Lingered. And then, just when Carly's breathing began to quicken and her toes to curl, it ended.

She'd been a part of him—fleetingly—and now she was alone again. She squelched a whimper. She couldn't quite uncurl her toes.

'I think it was,' Piran said raggedly. 'But I'm not sure. I think I'd better try that again, don't you?'

He didn't wait for her response, but instead ducked his head once more and melded his lips with hers. His hands came up this time, taking hold of her arms, drawing her into his, slipping around her and bringing her against him so that from lips to knees their bodies touched.

Carly felt a quiver run through her. Her own hands, which had been curled as tightly as her toes, slackened and came up around him, sliding under the cotton knit of his T-shirt to press against his hard, warm, muscular back.

Folly? Probably. Carly didn't know any more. All sense of self-protection, all rationality had deserted her. She was at the mercy of her need—and her love—for Piran St Just.

'It's not enough,' Piran said against her lips. 'It's so good, but it could be so much better.' She heard urgency in his tone now. The teasing was overlaid by a desire that sent tremors through him, but he made no move to steer her out the bathroom and toward the bed. 'Carly?'

'Wh-what?' Stop talking! she wanted to shout at him. Her nails dug into his back.

'Do you want me?'

'What do you think?'

He grimaced. 'I think you'd better. But if you don't I need to know now. I'll stop.' He gave her a rueful look. 'I can stop these days. I'll wait till we're married if that's what you want. It's up to you.'

She lifted her gaze to meet his. 'I want you,' she whispered. I love you, she told him in her heart.

He took her hand and drew her with him into the darkened bedroom, flipping off the bathroom light switch as he went. 'Here?' he asked. 'I've got a bigger bed in my room.'

'Do we need a bigger bed?'

Piran gave her a lopsided smile. 'No.'

'Then here's fine.'

There was a certain poetic rightness to it, she realized as she moved to lie down on the bed and reached for his hand to draw him down beside her. This had been her room during the times that she had come down here as a teenager. This had been the bed in which she'd lain while she'd entertained her adolescent fantasies.

She remembered how the moon had hung above the trellised bougainvillaea, spilling its cool light over her heated body as, night after night, she'd imagined loving Piran and Piran loving her.

And now he was here.

He was tugging his shirt over his head and tossing it on the floor. He was planting an arm on either side of her and settling his knees astride her thighs. His fingers were easing up the hem of her gown, exposing more of her thighs. She trembled at his touch, marveled at the intensity in his face.

She lifted her hands and touched his chest, raking her fingers lightly down through the dusting of dark hair that arrowed toward his navel. The muscles tightened at her touch. He bit down on his lip and she saw a shudder run through him.

'Careful,' he said, and his voice was unsteady. 'We're going to do this right.'

'Whatever you do will be right, Piran.' She touched him again, brushed her palm against his belly, slid her fingers just beneath the waistband of his cut-offs.

'Carly!' He sucked in his breath sharply.

She smiled. Folly? Oh, no doubt. But it was a dream come true to touch Piran like this, to make him quiver and hear the catch in his voice, the urgent strangled sound at the back of his throat.

He shifted again so that now his knees were between hers. His hands slipped beneath the sheer fabric and pushed it up past the thin barrier of her panties, across her belly, over her breasts. His thumbs grazed her nipples and a shiver skated down her spine. Her breath caught in her throat.

He urged her up so that he could slip the gown over her head and in the same motion tossed it to the floor to lie beside his shirt. His eyes never left hers until he hooked his thumbs in the elastic of her underwear. Then he bent his head, watching intently as he slowly stripped away this last garment and Carly lay naked before him.

Slowly, deliberately, he drew his hands down and cupped her breasts, traced circles on her skin, making her quiver and twist. With her fingers she grabbed handfuls of the sheet. He smiled. His hands moved on down, outlining the curve of her hips, then coming together at the downy apex of her thighs. His thumb teased her heated flesh. Her eyes widened. Her jaw clenched. He touched her again, stroked her.

'Piran!'

Her fantasies had never been this explicit. Oh, they'd been naked together, but somehow their clothes had melted away, not been removed with such exact care, such disturbing caresses. And, while they'd touched in her dreams, she'd never imagined a jolt like the one she felt when Piran's fingers actually touched her.

And besides his touch it was even more intimate because he was watching her reactions. Never in all her dreams had she and Piran looked at each other so hungrily; never had they devoured each other with their eyes.

'Not fair,' Carly whispered now, stunned at the shakiness of her voice. 'I want to see you too.'

Piran's mouth twisted. 'By all means.' His hands went to the buttons on his cut-offs, but Carly's reached out to still them.

'My turn.'

He looked for an instant as if he might protest. But then his mouth twisted further and he straightened up, kneeling tall between her legs. 'Whatever you say. Go ahead. Have your way with me.'

Carly smiled. 'I think I will.'

She couldn't believe she'd said it, let alone meant it.
But once the words were out she knew that when dreams
came true, folly or not, a woman made the most of them.

Carly had dreamed for years of loving Piran right here
in this bed. Now that she had the chance, she was going
to enjoy every minute of it.

She took her time. She didn't start at once with the
buttons. Instead, with a daring she hadn't known she
possessed, she let her fingers drop down to his knees,
then they drifted back up, tracing, teasing, touching
lightly the hair-roughened insides of his thighs, brushed
the scraggly cut-off fringe of his shorts, moved up briefly
beneath it, then slid down and began their trip all over
again.

As her hands made their upward journey, Piran's jaw
tightened. He shifted slightly, spreading his legs a bit
more, allowing her more access. She went higher, slid
her fingers right beneath the hem of his briefs, touched
him, caressed him with her fingers, traced him lightly
with her nails.

He moaned. 'Carly!' Her name was an explosion of
breath.

She looked at him worriedly. 'Aren't I doing it right?'

'Too damn right! You're torturing me.'

She laughed. 'And myself.'

'Then let's get on with it!' His hands went to the
buttons again, but she forestalled him, easing them open
herself, one by one, slowly, carefully. Her fingers felt
the heat of him pulsing through the thin cotton of his
briefs. He held very still until the last button came
undone and she peeled the cut-offs down his hips. Then
he practically scrambled out of them, yanking his briefs
off with them and pitching them both aside.

She had seen Piran naked before—the first night she'd
arrived and he'd hauled her up from the beach. That

man had been fierce and intimidating. This man was beautiful.

She said so and was met with an embarrassed laugh.

'I think that's my line.' He nuzzled her between her breasts, suckled each in turn, driving her wild. She gripped his shoulders desperately. Her legs shifted against his. Then his fingers went once more between her thighs and touched the core of her.

'Piran!' She reached for him, touching him too, needing to kindle flames in him that burned as brightly as those he was stoking in her.

'Now?' His voice was ragged.

'If you—are you——?'

He gritted his teeth. 'God, yes!' And then he became part of her at last.

It was pain and pleasure, desire and fulfillment, fantasy and reality all rolled into one. There was, too, one instant in which Carly's body resisted and panic flared in Piran's eyes.

'Carly?' He gazed down at her, shocked.

She laced her fingers against his back and drew him deeper. That was her answer.

Apparently it was enough, for after a moment's hesitation Piran began to move, slowly at first, so slowly that she thought she would die of frustration. Then his movements became faster, his breathing quickened into short, shallow gasps and her own matched it. Her fingers dug into his back, her thighs locked against his hips. Even their hearts seemed to pound in unison.

Once years ago Carly had gone bodysurfing. She knew the powerful building of the surf around her. She knew the sensation of having her body lifted by the surge of the wave and remembered the thrill of becoming a part of that flow of energy. Mostly she recalled the joy, the excitement of her headlong fall over the crest into the rush of the wave on to the shore.

That memory was as near as she could come to what she felt as she and Piran moved and crested and fell together. It didn't even come close.

He collapsed against her and she held him tight, reveling in the weight of his body on hers, in the warmth of his breath against her cheek, in the dampness of his sweat-slick back beneath her hands.

I love you, she told him in her mind, in her heart. Heaven help me, I love you, Piran St Just.

He lifted his head and their eyes met in the moonlight. His expression was grave. 'Why didn't you say?'

She knew what he was asking, and it wasn't about love. 'That it was my...' She faltered.

'First time,' he finished for her. 'Why didn't you?'

'Are you angry?'

'Of course not. I mean... Hell!' He looked more upset than angry. 'I wouldn't have just—just—— I would have taken more time,' he said finally. 'Tried to make it better for you.'

Carly smiled. 'It gets better?' There had been a moment's pain, but she certainly had no complaints about what had come after.

Piran gave a shaky laugh. 'Not for me. But I would...I could make it better for you.' He levered himself out of the bed. 'Wait right here.' He looked at her worriedly, as if she might vanish on him.

'I'm not going anywhere,' Carly assured him. A grin flickered over his face as he disappeared into the bathroom and came back moments later with a damp cloth and towel.

Gently—'The way I should have done if I'd known,' he muttered—he parted her thighs and bathed her, then dried her with equal care. His touch was so tender that it made her shiver with longing and she was astonished to find herself becoming aroused again.

She moved restlessly and Piran cocked his head, looking at her. 'Do you want...?' he began, then stopped, shaking his head doubtfully.

But Carly had no doubts.

'You. I want you,' she told him, and reached for him once more.

Carly awakened to the sun spilling across her bed. She sat bolt upright and stared at the clock. *Ten-forty*?

It couldn't possibly be. She *couldn't* have slept that late!

And then she realized that, yes, in fact she could have—because she remembered how she'd spent the night, and it hadn't been sound asleep.

But surely Arthur——?

She scrambled out of bed, starting toward his room, then realized something else: that she didn't have a stitch on.

Her nightgown lay on the floor where Piran had tossed it. Her panties were a few feet away from it. Piran's shorts and shirt—and Piran himself—were nowhere to be found.

Hurriedly Carly dressed in shorts and a sleeveless top. Then she washed her face and teeth and dragged a brush through her hair. She caught a glimpse of her face in the mirror and blushed. She looked so...so...*loved*.

Well, maybe that wasn't quite the right word. But her lips seemed somewhat fuller, felt slightly tender. Her breasts seemed sensitive against the sheer fabric of her bra. And the rest of her... Her color deepened and hastily she turned away, heading out to find out why Arthur hadn't roused her with his usual six-thirty babbling.

She found him in the living room sitting in Piran's lap, with Piran using Arthur's index fingers to type letters on the keyboard. At the sound of her feet on the plank floor, they both turned.

Arthur crowed cheerfully and Piran smiled.

'Sleeping Beauty has arisen,' he told Arthur.

Whatever color had vanished from Carly's cheeks came flooding back. 'I'm sorry. I didn't hear him,' she babbled. 'What time did he wake you?'

'A little after seven.'

'I should have——'

'No. You need your rest. You were very busy last night.' The smile turned into a grin.

'So were you,' Carly retorted, blushing.

Piran laughed. 'And I enjoyed every minute of it. Let's just say this morning was on me. Want some coffee?'

'Thanks. Yes.' What she really wanted was a refuge from the look in his eyes, which were already this morning warm with desire—which made her desire him again too. She went into the kitchen and poured herself a cup from the pot he'd made. 'Shall I bring you one?' she called, and was startled when he said from right behind her,

'Yes, but I'll drink it in here.' He was carrying Arthur and the similarity in their features seemed even more striking than usual this morning. Perhaps it was because Piran looked comfortable holding him now. Whatever it was, it made Carly smile.

'Is that for me or for him?' Piran asked her, taking the cup she handed him. Their fingers brushed. The electricity was still there.

'Is what for you?'

'The smile.' His eyes were hooded, but there was a gentleness in his expression that increased her self-consciousness.

'For both of you,' she said quickly. 'Of course.'

'Of course,' Piran said, his tone slightly mocking, and Carly wondered if she'd hurt his feelings. Surely not.

'How much have you done this morning?' she asked him, wanting to talk about something else, something that wouldn't make her blush even more.

'A fair bit. It's all come together. I can probably finish if I get rid of my helper. Arthur doesn't type very fast.'

'You should have got me up.'

'You needed the sleep.' He smiled at her. 'And you looked beautiful.'

Embarrassed at his frankness, Carly looked away. 'You were very clever, entertaining him that way,' she said after a moment.

Piran laughed. 'Entertaining him, hell. He's got to earn his keep. I figure if I keep typing with him in five years he'll be able to do it on his own.'

'Good idea,' she said, taking Arthur out of his arms.

'I'm just full of good ideas,' Piran said. 'Want to hear a couple more of them?' There was enough suggestiveness in his tone to tell her what the ideas entailed even without explanation.

Carly blushed. 'I think we'd better get to work right now,' she said, settling Arthur on her hip. 'Or one of us should, anyway.'

'There's not much for you to do until I finish. Why don't you and Arthur decorate the Christmas tree?'

He nodded toward the table and for the first time Carly noticed the array of things lying on it.

Apparently he and Arthur had done more than type this morning. They'd laid out fishing flies and lures, some of which she remembered seeing Piran use when they'd come here years ago. There were seashells, including several that she and Arthur had brought back from their daily excursions to the beach. There were small portions of fishnet and the sea glass he'd given her the other day, which she'd set on the mantel in a place of honor. He'd also provided several bits of driftwood, some dried pods off one of the trees they passed on the way to the beach and, next to them, a carton filled with freshly picked deep red and coral and white hibiscus flowers.

'You'll have to change the flowers every day, but as far as the rest goes...' Piran hesitated. 'I know it's not exactly your garden variety Christmas decorations, but Arthur and I thought maybe you could use some of it.' He spoke offhandedly as he carried his coffee into the living room and went back to the computer.

Carly stared at his back, then at the assortment of decorations he'd so carefully provided. For a man who hadn't even wanted a tree, he'd done an awful lot. Her heart felt suddenly very full. She hugged Arthur close.

'Yes, I will,' she said to Piran. 'Who wants a garden variety Christmas tree? This is a wonderful idea.'

Hanging lures and net and such on the tree with Arthur in one arm wasn't easy, but Carly wasn't complaining. In fact she would have happily sung out loud if she hadn't thought that the noise would bother Piran as he worked. She tried to move quietly, talking to Arthur only in an undertone as they hung the various ornaments.

Piran typed as if possessed, stopping only rarely, but smiling at the tree—and at her and Arthur—when he did so.

'It looks great,' he told her when at last she was done and stepped back to consider it.

'It does,' Carly agreed, smiling. She loved it. She remembered thinking last year that the tree she and her mother and Roland and his girls had decorated with brightly painted wooden nutcrackers and glass bells and papier-mâché angels was the most wonderful tree in the world. But it didn't hold a candle to this one, with its tiny colored lights, its gaily feathered lures and flies, its bits of polished glass and curling shells and smooth pieces of driftwood.

Piran flicked on the printer and got to his feet. As the pages spewed forth, he came over to stand behind Carly who still held Arthur in her arms. Piran slipped his arms around both of them and bent his head forward so that his lips just brushed the back of Carly's ear.

'I like it,' he said.

'Yes.'

His lips nibbled her ear. 'I like you.'

Carly smiled. 'I'm afraid I'm getting rather fond of you, too,' she said. I love you, her heart said again. But still the words remained unspoken. They had a start. She was afraid to push for too much.

'Ouch,' Piran said as Arthur reached up and grabbed his nose. 'Hey, kid, behave yourself.'

'He wants to be included,' Carly said.

'He is,' Piran asserted, prying the baby's fingers off his face and nibbling them until Arthur giggled. 'After all,' he added gruffly, 'he caused it.'

Right after lunch Piran said to Carly, 'We're going Christmas shopping.'

She looked up from the chair where she'd just settled down with the last chapter. 'Now? But I can't. I've got to finish this.'

'I meant Arthur and me. You're staying here.'

'But I saw this darling little wooden toy sailboat in the hardware store. We could hang it on the tree and then when Arthur gets a little bigger he could take it in the bath.'

'I'll look at it,' Piran promised.

'But——'

'You work. And if you finish, then we can celebrate tonight.' He waggled his eyebrows at her and she knew what kind of celebrating he had in mind. He looked pleased when the color rose in her cheeks. Carly wished she knew if it was just the idea of making love or of making love with her that caused his eagerness.

She smiled at him. He bent down and kissed her lingeringly on the lips.

'In fact,' he said when he'd left her breathless, 'we can take a few days off, then do the last run-through after Christmas. How about it?' He took Arthur from her with newly developed ease and started toward the door.

'I'd like that,' Carly admitted.

Piran nodded. 'It's a date.'

'You can leave Arthur with me this afternoon,' Carly called after him. 'You don't have to take him along.'

He turned back. 'No. The book is going to get your undivided attention. And Arthur is going to get mine. Aren't you, sport?'

It was a sign of how much he'd changed, Carly realized, that he seemed actually to be looking forward to it.

'A little male bonding?' Carly teased.

Piran grinned. 'You better believe it.'

The odd thing was, he meant it. And he was enjoying it. It surprised him how much he was enjoying Arthur.

It didn't surprise him how much he was enjoying Carly.

Talk about bonding! He grinned now as he walked back from town, carrying a sleeping Arthur, his thoughts busy reminiscing about how well they had bonded last night.

He'd been shocked to find out that Carly was a virgin. He was also pleased, though he knew very well he had no right to be. Still, it made him feel more responsible than ever to be considerate, attentive, the best lover she could ever wish for. He wanted to make up to her in quality what she would be lacking in quantity when she married him.

Well, actually, he thought with a grin, he'd be happy to provide the quantity too.

He was looking forward to doing a bit more bonding tonight after Arthur was tucked up in bed. They could go to bed right after he did. They'd have more time now that the book was pretty much under control. Just thinking about spending hours in bed with Carly made him hot. No surprise there.

What did surprise him was the fact that the longer he thought about it, marrying her made more and more sense.

It had been a spur-of-the-moment thing, what he'd told Wendy about being married to Carly. It had been stupid in the extreme. But once he'd said it the idea of actually marrying Carly hadn't seemed stupid at all.

It made sense. Piran had never really thought about getting married and having kids with her or anyone else. He'd known since he was a boy what he'd wanted to do with his life, and marriage and kids had never seemed a part of it. He wasn't against the idea. He'd just always been too busy.

Besides, what sort of examples had he had?

His own parents, from his earliest memories, had always seemed distant and preoccupied, their marriage a mystery. After their divorce, his mother had ceased to be part of his life, and Piran had expected his father to pursue his career with equally monkish fervor.

Arthur St Just's unexpected marriage to the very unsuitable Sue had rattled him thoroughly. It hadn't made sense and it had destroyed his rapport with his father.

Marriage had seemed to him something to stay well away from.

When Carly had taken it for granted nine years ago that if he wanted to make love to her he must want to marry her, he'd been aghast. And he'd rejected the notion—and Carly—out of hand.

Now he didn't.

Now he was mature. Ready to settle down. Plus he had a son who needed a mother.

Carly would be a good mother. She'd proved that. Besides, she liked to dive, she edited books and he loved to make love with her. What more could he possibly ask for?

Yes, marrying Carly now made a hell of a lot of sense.

He said as much to Arthur as he carried the child up the last few yards of the gravel road that led toward the house. Arthur sucked his thumb and sighed contentedly, nestling his head against Piran's shoulder. There was no doubt in Piran's mind that Arthur agreed with him.

As he approached the veranda he saw that Carly wasn't alone. There was a woman sitting on the swing. She had long, golden-brown hair and an island tan and looked vaguely familiar.

Across from Carly, he saw Des.

Piran's jaw tightened. Trust Des to show up the minute all the work was done.

At the sound of his footsteps they all looked up.

'You're back,' Carly said, and the expression on her face puzzled him. She looked as if she had sunstroke. Her eyes were dazed, her cheeks were flushed, yet there was a hint of white around her mouth.

The woman in the swing leaped to her feet and ran down the steps toward him. 'A.J.!' she cried, and if Piran hadn't hung on she would have snatched Arthur right out of his arms.

His eyes narrowed. 'Who the hell are you?'

'That's Angelica.' Carly smiled wanly. 'Arthur—er—
A.J.'s mother.'

Piran stared at the tawny-haired woman. She was
familiar, yes, but——

'Now wait a minute. I might have been round the bend
for a while, but I know damned well I never slept with
her!'

'No, you didn't,' Des said.

Piran's gaze jerked toward his brother who was getting
to his feet.

'I did,' Des said.

'What are you talking about?'

But Des only had eyes for the child in Piran's arms,
and his voice, when he spoke, was as soft as his smile.
'You're not his father—I am.'

# CHAPTER TEN

PIRAN supposed that if he made them go over it again and again someday he might feel less betrayed, might even feel he'd been given a reprieve.

At least he might feel it made sense.

'I can't believe you would just abandon your child on a veranda!' he said to Angelica for the second time.

Carly would never do a stupid, irresponsible thing like that, and she wasn't even Arthur's—he couldn't bring himself to think of the baby as A.J.—mother.

'I didn't think I was abandoning him!' Angelica retorted hotly. 'I thought Des was here. He'd made such a point out of telling everyone this was where he *had* to be so you two could finish your damned book!'

Des looked decidedly uncomfortable at her words. Piran thought he ought to look as if he was being consumed by the fires of hell.

'How did I know you were going to leave me a baby?' Des demanded. 'It isn't like you ever told me we were going to have one!'

'I tried,' Angelica said. 'You were never where I could get hold of you! You were always off on some boat or running around the world. If you had a phone—or an office—like a normal person——'

'Sorry!' Des snapped. Then immediately his tone softened and he reached out and took her hand. 'Hey, we've been through all this.' He looked at his brother. 'I'm sorry about the mix-up. She did try. And then, when she got desperate, she came here.'

'And left him! She could have waited,' Piran pointed out. 'I'd have been happy to tell her you were off sailing the seven seas.'

'Yes, well, she was annoyed by then. She thought I was avoiding her, avoiding responsibilities. She thought maybe a little shock treatment might make me see the light.' He gave a wry grimace. 'So she left him and took off to crew for Jim. Imagine her surprise when, the day after Jim picked her up, he sent her down into the cabin to take care of the mate with the flu and she found out it was me!'

'Imagine,' Piran said drily.

'You should have heard her when she thought I was here learning how to be a father and I was actually half a world away with no idea what she'd done.' Des shook his head in dismay at the memory.

Piran didn't have to hear her. He could imagine that too. What he couldn't imagine was life without Arthur.

To be fair, the past few weeks didn't seem to have been easy for Angelica either. The way she was cuddling Arthur in her arms right now, as if she couldn't bear to put him down, he knew she must have gone spare when she'd realized there was no way for her to get off Jim's boat at once and fly halfway round the world to the child she'd left on the veranda.

And then she'd had to explain to Des why she was so frantic. That couldn't have been easy either. Nor could their plight have made poor, unsuspecting Jim's shake-down sail any easier for all concerned.

So what? Piran thought savagely. It served them right!

It would have served them right if he and Carly had disappeared with Arthur and left no trace. He glared now at them both.

'We got married as soon as we could,' Des said. 'Somehow I never thought I'd spirit a woman off to Las

Vegas, but I did. And then we came right on here. We're really grateful,' he added. 'To both of you.'

He turned his gaze directly on Carly. 'I'm sorry. I had no idea when I asked you,' he apologized. 'You must hate me. First the book, then Piran, then A.J.' He grimaced sympathetically.

Piran's teeth clenched. His gaze followed Des's to see Carly's reaction to that.

She was smiling wanly. 'It's...all right,' she said softly.

She didn't say anything else. She had said almost nothing at all since he'd come back almost an hour ago. Apparently she'd already heard the explanations before he got there. At least she'd had no questions this time through.

He'd had a thousand, all furious. And all the while he'd been asking them Carly had simply sat there, motionless, her hands folded in her lap, her eyes either on them or staring off unseeing at the horizon.

'I don't think you ought to have a baby,' he snarled at Des and Angelica now. 'An irresponsible pair like you!'

Angelica gasped, cuddling Arthur closer and looking fearfully to Des to defend them.

Des did. He bristled. 'And I suppose you're more responsible?' One brow lifted. 'Who thought Arthur was probably his?' he said mockingly.

Piran flushed, then felt a stab of surprise when Carly spoke up.

'He didn't,' she said in a low, firm voice. 'He never thought that. Not from the first.'

'Not *at* first,' Piran corrected her. 'But then . . . well, I thought it was possible,' he conceded, glancing her way, wondering why in heaven's name he was arguing with her.

'Well, he's not yours,' Des said firmly. 'He's ours.' He reached out a hand and brushed it across Arthur's hair. 'Our son,' he repeated softly. His voice cracked on the words, but he didn't even seem embarrassed by the display of emotion, and that, finally, more than all the protestations he'd made so far, convinced Piran that his brother meant every word.

He sat in stunned silence and saw his future slipping away. No one else spoke either. In the distance he could hear the surf hitting the sand, a frog near by under a coconut tree.

Just like yesterday. But nothing was as it had been yesterday. Nothing at all. And Piran couldn't sit here any longer and pretend that it was. He shoved himself to his feet. 'Congratulations,' he said abruptly. 'I hope you're very happy. It was a long walk back from town and I'm hot. So if you don't mind I think I'll go for a swim.'

He left without another word.

It might not have been the shortest engagement on record, Carly thought, but it was close.

Probably she should have been brave enough to stick around until Piran got back from his swim and bid him a pleasant farewell.

But even though she knew she should, knew as well that there would be no end to Angelica and Des's speculations if she left at once, still she packed her bags and did just exactly that.

She couldn't stay around and pretend that nothing had happened. She couldn't even bring herself to follow him down to the shore.

He hadn't asked her. And if she went, what would he say to her that she could possibly want to hear? Would she have to endure awkward protestations that he would marry her anyway? Desperate mumblings that might get him out of an engagement he no longer wanted?

No, thank you. Carly didn't need to hear what she already knew.

She wanted to go home.

'Tonight?' Des demanded. 'You want to leave tonight?'

'Not tonight,' Carly said. 'Now. There's a plane at six. If I go now, I can catch it. I mean, why stay around?' she said desperately. 'The manuscript is, to all intents and purposes, finished. At least, Piran's part is. I can do my part in New York. Besides,' she lied, 'I miss the city. I miss my friends. It's Christmas, Des,' she added plaintively.

She didn't know which of her pleas convinced him, but finally he shrugged. 'If that's what you want. I owe you big. But what about saying goodbye to Piran?'

'He won't care.' She didn't know whether she hoped that was true or feared it was.

'OK,' Des said at last. 'Good thing I borrowed Sam's moke. I can run you to town in that.'

'I'll be ready in five minutes,' Carly said. She was ready in less.

Des waited with her in the Quonset hut terminal until the plane arrived. He looked as if he wanted to apologize again, to explain things that as far as Carly could see could never be explained. Or if they could she didn't want to hear them.

She avoided his gaze, shifting from one foot to the other, watching the clock and then the doorway to the terminal, half afraid that Piran would come through it at any moment—though rationally she knew there was no reason why he should.

Rationally she was sure he would be grateful to come back and find that she was gone and that they would never have to face each other again.

Still, by the time the plane arrived, she had bitten her thumbnail down to the quick and had Des asking anxiously, 'Are you sure you're all right?'

'Fine. Just eager to get home.' Carly gave a nervous little laugh. 'I think I must have island fever. You know, feeling too hemmed in. I just want to get away!'

Des frowned. 'Did you and Piran——?'

'No!' Carly leaned forward and kissed Des lightly on the cheek, then turned and bolted toward the door that the other three passengers had already gone through. 'Bye.'

She didn't say how lovely his son was or how much she was going to miss him or anything else irrelevant but oh, so true. She just ran for the plane and scrambled up the steps, hugging the carryall with the manuscript against her chest.

Diana would be pleased. So would Sloan. She'd done her job. And that was, after all, what she'd come for. Not for Des or Arthur. Or, God help her, Piran. She swallowed hard. Her throat ached. She felt a stinging behind her eyes.

Editors don't cry, she told herself fiercely as the plane began to rumble down the runway.

At least, she hoped they didn't.

'What do you mean, she left?'

'Just what I said. She said you'd finished the book— at least, you had finished your part—so there was nothing to wait around for. I guess she still had some revising to do, but——'

'What the hell has that got to do with anything?' Piran glared at his brother. He couldn't believe what Des had just told him, even though the knot that was tying itself in his stomach meant that his emotions seemed to know instinctively that it was true.

He'd been gone for three hours. It was already dark by the time he'd walked the length of the damned beach, trying to sort out what had happened, trying to figure out what to do next.

He'd wished Carly had gone with him, talked to him, listened to him, but as he'd walked he'd told himself that maybe it was better that she hadn't. Maybe they both needed a little time alone before they decided what to do together.

Or so he'd thought. Apparently Carly had made the decision for him.

'She said you wouldn't care. The book is why she came. That's what it was all about.'

'Was it?' Piran's tone was scathing. She'd said he wouldn't care? He kicked at the slats of the deck railing, then jammed his hands into the pockets of his shorts.

Des watched him without speaking for a long moment. Then, 'I thought it was,' Des said quietly. 'Did something happen between you?'

'None of your damned business!'

'I only thought——'

'Then stop thinking! You're no good at it.'

'Look, Piran, I'm sorry. Sorry for sticking you with Carly. Sorry for the whole mess. I've told you, it's not like I knew about A.J.'

'Who? Oh, you mean Arthur? This has nothing to do with Arthur.'

'Then what the hell are you so upset about?' Des paused and considered his older brother narrowly. 'Did you do something to Carly?'

Piran hunched his shoulders. 'What the hell would I do to Carly?'

'Hurt her.'

'Of course not.' Unless you counted accusing her of being a gold digger, taking her virginity, and proposing a marriage of convenience so he'd have someone to take care of his bastard child.

Piran raked a hand through his hair. Hell, no wonder she'd wasted no time getting out of there!

Once Arthur's identity had been resolved and any obligation she might have felt toward him thus relieved, the weight of the world must have dropped from her shoulders.

Obviously Arthur had been the attraction, not him. She hadn't wasted any time dumping him. He felt a hard, heavy ache somewhere deep inside that he didn't wholly comprehend.

It didn't make sense. He told himself he should be feeling relieved as well. He was well off out of such a marriage of convenience.

It wasn't as if he really wanted to marry Carly O'Reilly. Was it?

Carly made herself buy a Christmas tree. It was the day before Christmas Eve and the tree was the last one sitting by the grocery on the corner of 92nd and Broadway, and it was really pretty dreadful-looking. She told herself she felt sorry for it, that she needed to give it a home for the holiday.

But she wasn't sure if she was feeling sorrier for the tree or for herself.

It's what you wanted, she reminded herself hourly. You were the one who wanted not to have family around at Christmas. You could have gone to Roland's. You could still go to John's. He'd renewed his offer only the night before.

But she didn't want any of them.

She only wanted Piran.

She wanted the dream to go on, wanted to wake up and find herself in his arms, loving him, holding him, planning a future with him and with Arthur.

Ah, Arthur.

What a shock it still was whenever she thought about Des and Angelica's arrival, their startling revelation.

She thought about it all the time, mulled it over, wondered at the workings of providence. What would Piran have done if Des and Angelica had come later? Too late? After he and Carly had married?

Thank God that hadn't happened. She couldn't have borne it, knowing that he was trapped and it wasn't even his fault.

But she didn't seem to be bearing this much better.

'Hey, lady, you're gonna wreck that tree dragging it through the slush!'

Carly turned to see a rough-looking teenage boy leaning against a lamppost, watching her. He shoved himself upright as he spoke and came toward her. Carly glanced around nervously.

'How far you goin'?' he asked as he took it from her and hoisted it on his shoulder.

'Er, the other side of Amsterdam. Halfway up the block. It's fine, really. I——'

'Lead on.'

And what else could she do with him standing there with her tree on his shoulder?

He carried it all the way to her stoop and up the steps. There he stopped.

'I won't carry it in for you. Wouldn't want to make you too nervous.' He grinned and sketched her a quick salute. 'Merry Christmas.'

And before Carly could do more than stare after him he'd bounded down the stairs and headed back down the street.

'M-merry Christmas,' Carly called after him, still astonished at the uncalled-for good deed.

She thought about it. It made her smile—the first smile she'd managed since she'd got home three nights before.

'Things are looking up,' she promised herself. But by the time she had wrestled the tree up three flights of stairs she wasn't quite so sanguine.

Still, she did her best to muster some holiday spirit. She put on a CD of cheerful seasonal music—and if it didn't have any of the songs on the tape she'd left in Conch Cay that was all right too. Then she vacuumed her carpet using pine air-freshener beads in the vacuum. Finally she set up the tree in front of the window overlooking the garden four floors below.

She'd bought two strings of lights at the drugstore by the subway stop, and she was just getting them out of their boxes when the phone rang. She picked it up.

'Last chance,' a cheerful masculine voice said.

'Oh, John, I can't.'

'Of course you can. I'm leaving in a couple of hours. You've got time to get ready. What else are you doing? You're finished with the book.'

'I still have some work to do on it,' Carly hedged. She probably could have finished it already. Probably *should* have. But she couldn't bring herself to let it go.

She'd taken the manuscript out of her carryall when she'd arrived back in the apartment three nights ago. She'd set it on the counter between the living room and her tiny kitchen where she passed it fifty times a day. So she would remember that she still had it and that it needed work, she told herself.

As if she could forget.

Sometimes she picked it up, intending to go through it one last time. Instead she stood staring out the window, holding it against her chest and rocking back and forth, hugging it to her the way just days ago she had hugged Arthur.

Arthur. Piran.

If she didn't have the manuscript to hold, it would all seem like a dream now. Perhaps she should be trying to convince herself that it was.

But she couldn't. It was real—all of it—too real. And the manuscript was the only thing she had left to show for it.

Unless you counted her broken heart.

'Come on, Carly, what do you say?'

'Oh, John, really, I can't. If I came with you, your parents would get the wrong impression.'

'That I like you? That you like me?'

'That we're serious about each other.'

'I am serious.'

'But I'm...' She stopped herself before she said the word.

'Not?' John said it for her. He sighed. 'You couldn't maybe muster a little seriousness?'

Carly could tell he was hurt though he was trying to sound offhand. 'You're a wonderful friend,' she told him, and meant it.

'Damned by faint praise.'

'No, truly. I'm very fond of you.'

'Even worse.'

'Merry Christmas, John,' she said gently.

'Merry Christmas, Carly.'

She stood holding the receiver for a long moment before she finally set it down. She might have been able to forget if she'd gone with him. She might have started looking forward instead of back.

She told herself she was a fool. Piran didn't love her. If she gave him proper encouragement, someday John might.

Did she want to end up an old maid just because the one man she'd ever loved only needed her as a convenience?

How pathetic was she, for heaven's sake?

Still, when the buzzer rang an hour later and she knew it had to be John stopping on his way out of the city to give her one very last chance, she still couldn't bring herself to throw some clothes in a bag and go with him.

In fact she couldn't even bring herself to go downstairs. He would leave if he didn't get an answer, she assured herself even though the buzzer sounded once again.

'Don't do this, John,' she muttered, huddling into the sofa. 'Please don't.'

But John apparently wasn't taking nothing for an answer. At that moment she heard the buzzer blast again. And again.

Carly got up off the sofa and went into the bathroom, turned on the water and put her hands over her ears.

Finally, after ten minutes, she shut it off and came out. Silence. She breathed a sigh of relief.

There was a knock on the door.

Damn! He must have rung everyone in the building and someone must have pressed the answering buzzer to let him in. Carly shoved her hands through her hair, then sighed and went to answer it.

'John, I told you, I'm not——'

It wasn't John.

'Piran?'

'In the flesh.' He had a duffel bag in his hand and he pushed past her into the room, scowling as he came.

'Who's John?' he asked her at the same moment that she asked,

'What are you doing here?'

They stared at each other, each waiting for the other to speak. Carly could have waited forever, so stunned was she at the sight of him.

Piran was far more impatient. He glared at her. 'Shut the damned door and tell me who John is.'

Numb, Carly did, then leaned against the door, grateful to have something to hold her up.

'Well?' Piran prompted.

'He's a friend,' she said faintly. What are you doing here? Tell me! she wanted to shout at him.

'A good friend?'

'Yes. Why?'

'Have you slept with him?'

'*What*?'

A dull red flush crept up Piran's neck. He shoved a hand through his hair. He dropped the duffel bag and paced around her small living room. 'Forget it,' he muttered.

'I will not forget it,' Carly said, incensed. 'How can you ask me that after you... after you and I...?'

'I know, I know!' He kicked at the carpet. 'That's why I said forget it!'

Carly wasn't likely to, but she pressed her lips together in a tight line and composed herself. 'All right. I answered your question. Now you answer mine. Why did you come here? What do you want?'

'You left.' The bleak tone of his words surprised her. She looked at him closely.

'I thought you'd be glad.'

He frowned. 'Why should I be?'

'Well, once Des and Angelica showed up, you were free... of Arthur at least. But you still had me.' She shrugged awkwardly. 'I didn't want to hang around to listen to you tell me the engagement was off, thank you very much. I mean, it isn't as if you really wanted to marry me!' She blinked rapidly, hating the way her eyes were filling with tears.

'No,' he said softly. He bent his head, and whatever hope she'd held in one tiny corner of her heart that he might deny it died with that one word.

She swallowed painfully. 'So... what's the problem?'

Piran hesitated, then let out a harsh breath. 'The problem is I do now.'

The words were spoken so quickly that Carly wasn't sure she heard them—or, if she had, if she'd heard them right.

'What?' she asked after a moment.

'I want to marry you now.' A corner of his mouth lifted. 'Ironic, isn't it? Nine years ago you wanted marriage and I walked away. Then we agreed to it for Arthur's sake. And now, when Arthur doesn't need us any more, when he has his own set of parents at last, you walk away... and I can't.'

Carly just stared at him. 'Why can't you?' she said faintly. She wondered if she'd fallen asleep and started to dream. She looked around the apartment, trying to ground herself.

She saw the manuscript lying on the counter. She saw her scraggly Christmas tree still only halfway strung with lights. And she saw Piran St Just looking at her with a tormented expression in his eyes.

'Why do you think?' he said harshly.

Carly simply shook her head, not certain of anything now.

He gave a ragged half-laugh. 'You can't even imagine, can you, after all the good and sensible reasons for getting married that I gave you before?'

'Well, most of them seemed more to my benefit than yours,' Carly said cautiously. 'Besides Arthur and the editing. I mean, I'd get to go diving, travel, write books——'

'Make love?'

Carly felt her cheeks warm. 'That too,' she admitted.

'That too,' he echoed mockingly. 'God, you are well rid of me. I should never have come.' He started for the door, but she was blocking his way. 'Move.'

Carly stayed where she was.

'Why did you come, Piran?' she asked him quietly, barely daring to hope. 'Why do you want to marry me if not for Arthur?'

His throat worked. He rocked back and forward on his heels. 'For the time-honored reason, I suppose,' he said bitterly when the silence had dragged on far too long. 'Because I love you, damn it!'

He glared at her as if defying her to dispute it. She wasn't about to. She started to smile.

'That's right, go ahead and laugh,' he snarled. 'And then go off with this John character. I don't care. Just move out of my way!'

'No.' She met his gaze defiantly. 'And you do care. You just admitted it.'

'So now we're even.'

'Yes, we are.' Carly nodded slowly. 'Because I love you too.'

As she spoke the words she pushed away from the door at last and crossed the few feet that separated them. She slid her arms around him, and Piran groaned as her hands locked against his back and her lips lifted to touch his.

It was a kiss as hungry and eager and passionate as the ones they'd shared on her birthday nine years before.

It was a kiss as sweet and tender as the ones he'd given her after they'd made love just days ago. It was ecstasy.

And it was agony when Piran finally broke it moments later to ask raggedly, 'You're not just saying that, are you?'

Carly laughed. 'Does it feel like it?'

'No, but—God, Carly, by rights you ought to hate me. Are you sure?'

'I think I'm the one who ought to be asking that question. I've loved you for years. You didn't love me last week.'

Piran smiled wryly. 'I did. I just didn't realize it. I never admitted it to myself. Not until after Des came and robbed me of my excuse for marrying you, that is.' He met her gaze and held it and Carly saw in his eyes everything she'd ever hoped to see.

She touched his cheek. 'Do you need an excuse?' she asked him softly.

'Not any more.' He kissed her again and showed her what he meant with his lips as well as his words. 'I have the best one of all and the only one that matters: I love you.'

'Oh, Piran!' She hugged him tightly, kissed him back, and didn't object in the least when his fingers fumbled open the buttons of her shirt and made quick work of sliding down the zipper of her jeans. As she led him into the bedroom, she was busy doing the same to him.

'Do you have a thing about Christmas trees?' Piran asked her late the next morning as she was making him toast and coffee. They were both in her tiny kitchen, stepping on each other's feet and getting in each other's way, but it really didn't matter because it simply gave them more excuses to touch and kiss.

'I like them. Why?'

'Well, you dragged that one home on Conch Cay. And I notice you've got one half dressed over there.' Piran nodded in the direction of the tree that Carly had never finished putting lights on the night before because she and Piran had had far more interesting things to do.

'Maybe I do have a thing about them,' Carly said now, considering the tree and the possibility. 'They remind me of the good things in life, the things people share—home and family and hope. I was having a hard time mustering it with this one, though,' she admitted, 'until you came.'

'I know what you mean.' He bent and fished in his duffel bag which sat beside the sofa, then he handed her a wadded-up beach towel. 'Open it.'

Carly set it down on the table and did just that. Inside it she found smaller towels. Carefully she opened each one. She found the fishing lures and flies that she'd hung on the tree in Conch Cay. She found the bits of sea glass, the shells, the pods, the fishnet and the driftwood.

She looked at him, amazed. 'You brought all the ornaments on the tree?'

'They were ours, not Des's and Angelica's. Our home and our family and our hope.' His voice was almost fierce in its intensity. He looked right at her. 'They have to make their own. They are. I told them how.'

Carly smiled. She laid her fingers against his cheek. His hand came up and wrapped around hers. He pressed a kiss into her palm.

'I didn't know what I was going to do with them when I took them,' he said after a moment. 'Des thought I was out of my mind. I was. It seemed a hell of a long shot bringing them here.' He hesitated, then asked, 'Can we put them on your tree?'

'Our tree,' Carly corrected him.

It took them most of the afternoon. And when they were finished Carly turned out the lights except for the ones on the tree, lit a pair of candles on the mantel, then curled up next to Piran on the sofa. 'Isn't it beautiful?'

'Beautiful,' he agreed. 'But I think it needs a little something right over there.' He pointed to a bare spot.

'I can move the driftwood.' Carly started to get up.

But Piran caught her hand and pulled her back down. He reached into the duffel bag again and handed her a small sack.

'You put these where they belong.'

'What?' She opened the sack. In it were two even smaller wrapped packages. She looked at Piran. He nodded. She opened the first one. It was a small black velvet box. It held a ring. A diamond solitaire ring.

'I said I was going Christmas shopping.'

She started. 'But that was...that was before...'

'It was, but even then I didn't want any question about this being a legitimate marriage. I couldn't have said, but somewhere inside I knew. Will you wear it, Carly?'

And this time Carly didn't even bother to blink back the tears. 'Forever,' she promised.

He slid the ring on her finger, then kissed her. 'Open the other one.'

She fumbled with the wrapping, then opened a small cardboard box to draw out a tiny wooden object.

'It...it's Arthur's sailboat!' She lifted wide eyes toward Piran. 'But surely you should have left this for him?'

'I did. Every little boy should have a boat. But before I left I bought another one. Call it foolishness. Call it desperation. Call it love. But I was hoping,' he said, drawing her into his arms, 'as only a desperate man dares hope, that someday somehow I might be able to talk you into having an Arthur of our own...'

*Christmas Journeys*

# 4 new short romances all wrapped up in 1 sparkling volume.

Join four delightful couples as they journey home for the
festive season—and discover the true meaning of
Christmas...that love is the best gift of all!

A Man To Live For - Emma Richmond

Yule Tide - Catherine George

Mistletoe Kisses - Lynsey Stevens

Christmas Charade - Kay Gregory

**Available: November 1995**          **Price: £4.99**

## MILLS & BOON

# MILLS & BOON

## By Request

*Bestselling romances brought
back to you by popular demand*

Two complete novels in one volume
by bestselling author

# Robyn Donald

## Storm over Paradise
## The Stone Princess

Available: November 1995          Price: £3.99

# MILLS & BOON

## *Kids & Kisses—where kids and romance go hand in hand.*

This winter Mills & Boon brings you Kids & Kisses— a set of titles featuring lovable kids as the stars of the show!

### Look out for
### The Secret Baby by Day Leclaire
### Doctor Wentworth's Babies by Frances Crowne
### in November 1995 (Love on Call series).

Kids…one of life's joys, one of life's treasures.

Kisses…of warmth, kisses of passion, kisses from mothers and kisses from lovers.

In Kids & Kisses…every story has it all.

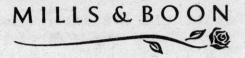

# MILLS & BOON

## Next Month's Romances

Each month you can choose from a wide variety of romance with Mills & Boon. Below are the new titles to look out for next month.

| | |
|---|---|
| DARK FEVER | Charlotte Lamb |
| NEVER A STRANGER | Patricia Wilson |
| HOSTAGE OF PASSION | Diana Hamilton |
| A DEVIOUS DESIRE | Jacqueline Baird |
| STEAMY DECEMBER | Ann Charlton |
| EDGE OF DECEPTION | Daphne Clair |
| THE PRICE OF DECEIT | Cathy Williams |
| THREE TIMES A BRIDE | Catherine Spencer |
| THE UNLIKELY SANTA | Leigh Michaels |
| SILVER BELLS | Val Daniels |
| MISTRESS FOR HIRE | Angela Devine |
| THE SANTA SLEUTH | Heather Allison |
| AN IRRESISTIBLE FLIRTATION | Victoria Gordon |
| NEVER GO BACK | Anne Weale |
| THE MERMAID WIFE | Rebecca Winters |
| SOCIETY PAGE | Ruth Jean Dale |